Suicide in Suffolk

AN UNLIKELY PAIR OF HEROES UNCOVER A SINISTER PLOT IN A QUIET COASTAL TOWN

D.Ayres

To my family, we've created many memories in Lowestoft

1

He lifted the lifeless body and placed it in the vehicle, the weight heavier today, both physically and emotionally. He'd encountered death countless times, but this one held a haunting secret. Lowestoft, the coastal town, lay eerily still. The bustling streets had vanished, replaced by an unsettling hush, broken only by distant crashing waves. Navigating the unlit road cautiously, he reached the desolate car park, unease knotting his gut, urging him on.

After parking near the entrance, he turned off the engine, slipped the keys into his pocket, and cast one last glance at the body before heading towards the building.

Peering through the glass, he saw only darkness, his reflection uneasy with questions. Would they understand, or would suspicion arise? His trembling hand mustered the courage for several firm knocks.

Despite numerous failed attempts and mounting frustration, he checked his pocket watch. The hands pointed to an ungodly early hour, evoking a quiet sigh. He trudged back to the vehicle with slumped shoulders and heavy steps, fumbling for the correct key.

Suddenly, a light flickered on behind him, casting light on the car park entrance. A lock turned, and a silhouette emerged at the building's entrance.

A woman's voice called out, 'Hello, is anyone out there?'

'I'd nearly lost hope,' the man replied. He continued toward the entrance, his shoes shuffling on the cracked pavement.

'Is everything okay, sir?'

Without answering, he looked around the car park and stepped into the light, closing the gap between them. Coming to a stop, he scrutinised her closely, noting her appearance.

'Not exactly, Miss.' He adjusted his bow tie. 'I'm here to report a crime!'

'I see, sir. Unfortunately we're closed right now, but you can come back when we open or report the crime on our website, and we'll investigate—.'

'I don't use the internet, you see. This is rather urgent. Can you perhaps make an exception and let me speak with someone right away?'

She scanned his clothes and face, offering a brief smile, as if assuring herself that he wasn't a threat.

'Okay, follow me,' she said whilst motioning for him to follow her.

He followed the young officer down the hallway, matching her pace. Occasionally, she slowed and glanced over her shoulder at him.

'We don't often have individuals showing up to report crimes at this hour.'

'I understand it's unusual, officer. But I promise you, what I have to say is of the utmost importance. Lives may be at stake.'

The officer hesitated for a moment, her eyes searching his face for sincerity.

'Alright, if you say so, sir. But remember, we take matters of this nature seriously. If you're wasting our time, there will be consequences.'

He hastened his pace to match the officer's stride, eager to convey the weight of his revelation.

The modest police station had narrow, plain-walled hallways. The woman led him to the office area. The air carried a mix of stale coffee and an unidentified aroma.

She halted at the end desk near the window. With a friendly smile, she grabbed a chair from another desk and gestured for him to sit. As he took a seat, he observed the perfectly tidy workspace, complete with family photos and neatly arranged files.

As she bent over to her desk drawer and straightened up with a notepad and pen in hand, a lock of dark brunette hair slipped across her face. She quickly brushed it behind her ear, revealing a pair of attentive green eyes.

'I'm PC Cooper. I need to gather some details for our incident log. Could you please provide your full name, age, and address?'

Collecting his thoughts, he replied, 'Cecil Whitford, June 11, 1952. My address is 70 Denmark Road, Lowestoft, NR32 2EQ.'

'Okay, Mr Whitford, you're reporting a crime. Can you describe what happened?'

Taking his time to reply, he said, 'I'm not too sure. I never actually witnessed the crime taking place.'

'I appreciate your willingness to come forward, Mr Whitford. Reporting a potential crime is an important step, even if you didn't witness it directly. Please take your time and provide as much detail as possible. We're here to listen and gather all relevant information.'

His hands clenched the chair's edge, his knuckles turning white from the pressure.

'I'm here to report a murder,' he finally confessed.

2

'A murder?' she asked.

He nodded.

'This is serious, Mr Whitford. Can you explain the situation? Let's start with the victim.'

'I don't have much information. She's not very talkative.'

Before she could utter another word, Mr Whitford pressed on, 'Let me take you to her. I've brought the body. It's just outside.'

'Wait! What? Are you saying you brought a dead body here?'

'Yes. I'm parked just outside.'

His words hung in the air, leaving her trying to piece together the situation. She remained composed, her training as a police officer guiding her to handle the situation professionally. 'Thank you for sharing this information, Mr Whitford.'

Mr Whitford's admission surprised her. She

couldn't dismiss it outright; instead, her duty as an officer compelled her to delve into this improbable situation.

'Follow me,' she instructed, gesturing towards the dimly lit hallway.

Their footsteps resonated ominously through the empty hallway. Pausing by a door, she struggled to steady her hand while attempting to unlock it.

'Please, have a seat.' She gestured towards the chairs in the room. 'I'll need to inform my boss about what you've said. I'll be right back.'

The room exuded austerity, furnished with a solitary table surrounded by four unadorned metal chairs. A single audio recorder, its soft hum the only disruption, rested on the bare table. The walls, cloaked in a drab shade of grey, seemed to absorb the room's lifelessness.

Mr Whitford strode to the table and took a seat, his movements deliberate. He folded his hands calmly on his lap. The fine lines etched on his face hinted at years of experience and stories untold. From the details he shared earlier, it was clear he had seen more than his fair share of life.

He was dressed smartly in a sombre suit and grey bow tie—the attire of someone who held respect for the solemnity of his profession. He remained facing her. She met his stare, her thoughts racing to untangle the enigma before her. Behind his composed exterior, what fears, regrets, or purpose lay hidden?

PC Cooper swiftly left the room, closing the door behind her in silence.

Wanting to verify Mr Whitford's words and take a break from the tense atmosphere inside, she walked to the car park.

In the dimly lit car park, her familiar white Fiat 500 sat alongside an unfamiliar, old-looking black vehicle.

Approaching cautiously, a sense of foreboding settled over her. Maybe it was just a prank, some attention-seeking ploy by an eccentric individual.

This had to be it. The rest of the car park lay deserted. She hoped for a false alarm, but her hope crumbled when a distinct shape caught her eye through the rear window. Drawing closer, PC Cooper peered through the glass and her eyes widened in disbelief. A body lay motionless inside the vehicle. She clenched her fists, her hands trembling involuntarily.

PC Cooper, who had devoted her life to upholding the law, felt her legs give way beneath her. She sank to the ground, overcome by a wave of shock and nausea. Her stomach revolted, expelling the remnants of her once-promising breakfast in a grotesque display on the pavement. She wiped her lips with a shaky forearm, taking a moment to steady herself before making her way back to the station.

The image of Mr Whitford haunted her. She wrestled with conflicting emotions, her curiosity warring with a sense of dread. What could drive a seemingly unassuming elderly man to commit such a heinous act? Why had he chosen to confess this to her?

Pausing outside Mr Whitford's holding room, PC Cooper strained to catch any sounds from within. Then, unexpectedly, his calm voice broke the silence, sending a shiver down her spine.

'Have you located her body?' His voice was steady, but it held a hint of anticipation.

3

PC Cooper's sense of duty propelled her into action, demanding both professionalism and urgency, no matter how unsettling it was. How could he be so calm after bringing a dead body to the police station? She maintained her composure, putting distance between herself and the man who seemed to be hiding something.

She hurried to her desk and called Sergeant Parker.

'Hello, Keeley. You're calling early. Is everything all right?'

Keeley took a deep breath. 'No, sir... something terrible has happened.'

'Are you okay? What is it? What happened?' Sergeant Parker's voice rose with concern.

'Well, I need to speak with you, sir. There's been a murder.'

'What!?' Sergeant Parker's voice reflected his

concern.

'—Are you still there, sir? What should we do?'

'Yes. Just give me a moment, Keeley. Let me think. Give me the address, I'll send Paul and Hannah right away. You also need to contact the coroner's office,' Sergeant Parker instructed.

'Sir, I'm already on the scene. There's a parked car here at the station, and there's a body inside.'

'Good Lord, Keeley!' Sergeant Parker gasped. 'Call the coroner right away. Stay where you are. Keep an eye out for any suspicious activity and wait for my arrival. How on earth did we end up with a murder at our own station?'

'Alright, sir. I'll do that. Please, hurry.'

Keeley ended the call. She then quickly dialled the coroner's office, ensuring they would be part of the investigation.

The minutes dragged on, each one amplifying the urgency that hung in the air. Moments later, footsteps echoed down the hall. Keeley looked up to see Sergeant Parker approaching in a rush. His round face bore a determined expression, and his bald head glistened under the ceiling lights. Already perspiring, he dabbed his forehead with a handkerchief.

'Keeley,' he said firmly. 'Did you call the coroner?'

'Yes,' she replied. 'But they won't be here for a few hours.'

'It's okay. I'm here now. Let's go look at the body,' he said.

Keeley led the way back to the car park, her steps urgent. As they approached the vehicle, Sergeant Parker peered into the back. His brows furrowed, and he shook his head slightly.

A low, frustrated utterance escaped his lips as he stepped back, 'Damn it.'

'I know, it's disturbing. I've never witnessed something like this before.'

'Jees, what the hell is this I've stepped in?' he grumbled.

Keeley pressed her lips together, her shoulders shaking slightly with suppressed amusement.

He walked over to the curb and scraped his boots in an attempt to remove the neon green vomit.

'Do we know how this car got here? It appears to be an old hearse. Maybe a local funeral home is missing a body?'

Keeley's eyes widened as she noticed something she had missed earlier—the vehicle was unmistakably a hearse. In the dim light, the details had been obscure, but now, with the sun rising higher, she could see the black paint showed signs of fading, and the vinyl top appeared clean but slightly worn. Its elongated form seemed out of place among the few other cars in the mostly empty car park, mainly occupied by police vehicles. In the soft morning light, the silver accents along its sides gleamed subtly.

She cleared her throat, 'I have an idea how it

ended up here.'

'Really? Tell me,' Sergeant Parker urged, his eyes fixed on Keeley.

'It belongs to Mr Whitford.'

Sergeant Parker's brows furrowed. 'Who's he? And why is his hearse parked here with a dead body in the back?'

Keeley took a breath before responding. 'Well, he drove it here this morning, sir. I'm currently holding him in meeting room one.'

The distant hum of traffic filled the air as Sergeant Parker let out a frustrated sigh.

'Alright, let's leave this here for the coroner when they arrive,' he said, gesturing towards the hearse. 'In the meantime, let's talk to Mr Whitford and figure out what the hell is going on.'

Keeley entered the building, leading the way to the interview room where Mr Whitford was held. Sergeant Parker followed closely, his presence reinforcing her resolve.

After unlocking the door, they stepped inside. Keeley focused on Mr Whitford. Her mind raced with questions and suspicions. His confident smile couldn't deter her. She knew there was more to him, and she was determined to uncover the truth.

Mr Whitford's eyes lifted as they entered. His face turned solemn as he spotted Sergeant Parker. 'I was starting to think you had forgotten about me.'

Keeley's eyes narrowed, and her voice carried a hint of steel. 'Thank you for waiting patiently, Mr Whitford. This is Sergeant Parker,' she said, gesturing towards her colleague. 'Based on what happened this morning and the body in your vehicle outside, we need to conduct a voluntary interview to aid our investigation.' The taste and smell of vomit resurfaced in her mouth.

Sergeant Parker examined Mr Whitford. He thought he recognised the man but couldn't remember where from.

'When you say voluntary, does that mean I can just leave?' Mr Whitford asked, narrowing his eyes.

Tension filled the room and heavy silence followed. Sergeant Parker and Mr Whitford exchanged looks, assessing each other's intentions.

'Yes, but if you don't cooperate, we may have to arrest you later to get the information we need for the investigation.'

'Fine. Let's proceed,' Mr Whitford replied calmly. He had been in a similar situation before with the police for his misjudgement and rash actions.

4

Sergeant Parker and Keeley felt uneasy as they sat down.

Switching on the tape recorder, Sergeant Parker broke the silence in the room, 'This interview is being recorded and may be used as evidence in a trial. It's May 16, 2023, at 9 a.m. I'm Sergeant Parker, and this is PC Cooper. Please state your full name and date of birth.'

'Cecil Whitford, June 11, 1952,' Mr Whitford replied.

'Before we proceed, I want to remind you of your right to seek free and independent legal advice. Would you like to consult a legal advisor now or have one present during the interview?'

Mr Whitford simply replied, 'No.'

'By law, we are required to ask for your reasons,' Sergeant Parker clarified.

'They are the most selfish species on the planet —need more reasons?' Mr Whitford's voice cut in. 'But I'm declining legal representation on the basis that I'm innocent, and I find it mildly amusing that I'm being considered a suspect.'

'I must caution you,' Sergeant Parker stated firmly. 'You have the right to remain silent or refuse to answer any questions. But if you later rely on something you don't mention now in court, it may harm your defence.'

'The interview is audio and visually recorded. Anything you say may be used as evidence. Do you understand?' Keeley asked.

Mr Whitford nodded.

'Let the record show, Mr Whitford is confirming by nodding his head,' noted Keeley.

'The purpose of this interview is to discuss the events that took place at precisely 6 a.m. this morning. You arrived at the Lowestoft police station, informing us about a murder. Then we found in the back of your vehicle a body. Let's start by going through the details together,' Keeley began. 'Firstly, could you confirm whether the vehicle in the car park belongs to you?'

'Yes, I've had Angel for over twenty years. She's a 1984 Rolls-Royce Silver Spur Hearse Conversion, quite rare these days,' he said.

'Angel?' questioned Sergeant Parker.

'Indeed. I've transported many bodies, hence her nickname. Do you know, I've never broken down in the thing or had so much as a scratch on it.'

Sergeant Parker confronted Mr Whitford with a serious expression. 'In your vehicle, currently parked out front of this building, is a female corpse! Can you tell us how this came to be?'

Mr Whitford's expression shifted, his jovial demeanour giving way to a serious one. 'Well, I put her there.'

Sergeant Parker raised an eyebrow, taken aback by Mr Whitford's blunt confession. 'You put her there?' he repeated incredulously. 'Why would you do that?'

'I'm certain there has been foul play at hand. I believe she was murdered!'

Sergeant Parker exchanged a puzzled glance with PC Cooper, who had been listening intently.

'Okay, Mr Whitford, indulge us,' replied Sergeant Parker, sounding unconvinced.

'I picked up the deceased, Miss Lizzie Hargrave, yesterday from the Ipswich Hospital mortuary. A mortuary technician mentioned her tragic bathtub suicide. I transported her to my funeral parlour in Angel, then moved the body to the crematorium's cool storage for preservation.'

He paused, running a hand through his thinning hair before continuing. 'Let me see... there was another body...yes! I had to deal with another body. It happened earlier in the morning, with some idiotic teenager driving those electric scooters you see around town. Only went and collided with a car. Nasty stuff indeed, suffered all sorts of terrible injuries.

Never made it through the night. Absolute death traps those scooters!'

'Can we stay focused on Miss Hargrave?' Sergeant Parker asked impatiently.

'Yes, where were we? After I returned to Miss Hargrave, I began to prepare her for embalming. You see, the family wanted to preserve the body for a few days so they could sort the funeral out. Of course, it all came as quite a shock.'

Mr Whitford briefly began explaining the embalming process, from firstly washing the body, then going into graphic details about how to make a small incision to drain the blood, and then finally injecting an embalming solution.

Keely's face twisted in disgust as she listened to Mr Whitford's description, struggling to keep down what was left of her breakfast.

'Mr Whitford, can we jump ahead? As interesting as this all is, I want to fast forward to the part where you believe that the victim was murdered!' Sergeant Parker said.

'All in good time, but if you insist. Well, there I was, in the midst of preparing the body, when a few irregularities caught my attention. First off, her mouth— it was tightly shut. Strangely enough, I couldn't see any external foam around her mouth, but I did find some in her nostrils. Those bruises on Miss Hargrave's wrists and under her armpits, they weren't glaringly obvious, but they were there, without a doubt. The way I see it, she was probably unconscious.

Somebody must've hauled her into the bath and then submerged her until she drowned.'

Sergeant Parker's eyes narrowed as he leaned forward in his seat. 'I find it surprising that a funeral director is so knowledgeable about what a victim of drowning looks like! What makes you so confident that someone else drowned her?'

'Experience and expertise.'

'Is that right?' sneered Sergeant Parker.

'Yes. A lifetime ago, I was a field medic in the Royal Navy. I only joined the family business later in life.'

'You were a field medic in the Royal Navy?' Keeley asked, raising an eyebrow. 'That's impressive.'

'I served all over the world,' he said proudly. 'I saw a lot of death and destruction, but I also witnessed immense courage and sacrifice. It was an experience that changed my life.'

'I understand,' Sergeant Parker said, nodding. 'And what leads you to believe that Miss Hargrave's death was a murder?'

'I've encountered numerous drowned bodies,' Mr Whitford asserted. 'The bruising on her wrists and beneath her armpits doesn't align with the typical marks from a bath suicide. It appears more consistent with someone holding her underwater.'

Keeley leaned closer, her eyes wide and her mouth slightly open. She couldn't help but hang on to every word Mr. Whitford said. Her brow furrowed in concentration as she pieced together his story, searching for any discrepancies.

Sergeant Parker looked on questioningly, his scepticism thinly veiled. 'That's a very interesting theory. We'll need to do some more investigating to see if there's any evidence to support it. How do we know the bruising didn't happen post-mortem, perhaps when they lifted her out of the bath or when you brought her here?'

'Your accusations are rather insulting, Sergeant. My family has been tending to the deceased for generations.'

'Okay, okay. Settle down, Mr Whitford,' Sergeant Parker remarked, raising his palm in a calming gesture.

Keeley stepped in. 'No offence was intended. We need to be thorough with our investigation. We will be sure to share your concerns regarding the bruising with the coroner when they arrive,' she said, keen to avoid the interview escalating and getting confrontational.

'Let's take a step back, Mr Whitford. I must admit, I find this entire scenario highly improbable. I mean, how did the killer gain entry? You mentioned there were no signs of defensive wounds, yet they managed to compel her to drown herself.'

'Well, I'm not entirely sure. It's a puzzling situation.'

Keeley's interest piqued even further as the

interview progressed. As he spoke, it became clear that there were several inconsistencies in his theory, raising questions about his credibility and the true nature of his involvement.

Sergeant Parker then posed another critical question, breaking the building tension. 'Well, how about an easier question to answer, Mr Whitford? For instance, why did you bring the body here instead of reporting it to the coroner's office?'

Mr Whitford looked around the room as he hesitated.

'I understand that this must have been a difficult situation for you, Mr Whitford,' Keeley said, 'But we need to understand the thought process that led you to bring the body here. Can you walk us through it? Maybe that will help us get a better grasp of your perspective.'

Mr Whitford visibly relaxed. Taking a deep breath, he began to explain, 'Well, I...I don't know,' he stammered. 'It just felt like the right thing to do. I didn't want to leave her there, you see. Not with...not with what happened to her.'

Keeley's eyes softened, her head slightly tilted. 'I see,' she said. 'It sounds like you were genuinely concerned for her well-being.'

Before Keeley could continue, Sergeant Parker interjected, his voice cutting through the room, direct and probing. 'What do you mean by that? What happened to her, Mr Whitford?'

Mr Whitford hesitated for a moment before

responding, his certainty wavering. 'I've already told you my theory. She was murdered, I'm sure of it.'

As Mr Whitford's story ended, Keeley was torn between intrigue and scepticism. The pieces of the story didn't fit well. Inconsistencies raised questions about Mr Whitford. She glanced at Sergeant Parker, and their shared moment of unspoken understanding confirmed her suspicions.

Sergeant Parker leaned forward, 'Mr Whitford, I need you to be completely honest with us,' he said. 'Did you have anything to do with her death?'

5

The room crackled with tension as everyone awaited Mr Whitford's response.

A sudden knock at the door interrupted their conversation. Keeley stood and approached the door, gently turning the knob before entering the dimly lit hallway.

'Are you and Sarge waiting for a coroner? He's arrived,' PC Seddon informed her.

'Yes, thank you,' Keeley replied promptly.

Keeley re-entered the room and approached Sergeant Parker. Leaning over, she whispered into his ear.

'Please bear with us for a minute, Mr Whitford. It's 9:45 a.m., and we'll conclude the interview now,' Sergeant Parker informed.

They walked to the front of the building. The solitary figure in the dark navy suit shifted awkwardly on the spot, adjusting a paisley tie.

Sergeant Parker extended his hand. 'Hello, I'm

Sergeant Parker, and this is PC Cooper.'

'Steven Baker, Assistant Coroner.' He shook both of their hands enthusiastically. 'You mentioned a body—are we driving in a police car to the scene?'

'That is not necessary. It's outside in the car park.'

Mr Baker's face contorted in disbelief. 'Outside? In the car park? You must be joking.'

Sergeant Parker didn't respond; instead, he turned, walked out into the car park and headed over to the vehicle he had inspected earlier.

Once they reached the vehicle, Mr Baker began circling it and scrutinising it closely.

'Watch your step. There's vomit on the floor there,' Sergeant Parker said sternly while pointing towards the grotesque, neon-green vomit alongside the vehicle.

The coroner sidestepped it to avoid it and scrunched up his face in disgust.

A small smirk formed at the corner of Keeley's lips.

'Can you unlock the rear and I'll have a quick look? What information do you have about the victim and how they got here?'

'The victim is Miss Lizzie Hargrave. She was brought here this morning by a local funeral director who is adamant she has been murdered.'

'Well, that answers my next question about why she's in a hearse.'

'Keeley, the keys!' ordered Sergeant Parker. He

was frustrated with the start of the morning and now with the obligations this body had put on him.

'I don't have them.'

Sergeant Parker's voice grew stern, 'What do you mean you don't have them? Well, where are they?'

'Oh no. They must be with Mr Whitford,' she said, realising her error.

'Keeley, you should have collected his belongings. That's a rookie mistake. I expect better from you.'

'I'm sorry, sir. At the time, he wasn't a suspect. I thought he was a bumbling old man wanting attention,' pleaded Keeley.

'Go get them right away!' commanded Sergeant Parker.

Flustered, she quickly turned and hurried back into the building towards the interview room.

As Keeley entered the room, her eyes fell on Mr Whitford, slouched in a chair with his head tilted back and eyes closed.

Her voice rose urgently, 'Hello, Mr Whitford. Please wake up!' He didn't stir. She shouted louder, 'Mr Whitford, wake up.'

No response. Keeley walked further into the room and slammed the door shut. Mr Whitford stirred but remained asleep. What a morning, she thought to herself. As she walked over to Mr Whitford, she shook him.

His eyes snapped open, and he looked bewildered.

'Where am I?' he asked, his voice groggy.

'Lowestoft Police Station, Mr Whitford. I'm PC Cooper. You brought a body here this morning.'

He looked at her blankly, then smiled and nodded.

'We need your car keys to examine the body.'

Mr Whitford fumbled through his pockets in search of the keys, eventually finding them and extending them towards her.

'Thank you,' Keeley said, she examined the keys in her palm as she took them from Mr Whitford. There were two keys, a silver hexagon-shaped key, a small gold Yale key, and a small square key ring that was scratched, but she could make out some words: 'Si vis Pacem, para bellum.' Latin perhaps, she thought to herself. Clutching the keys, she dashed back into the hallway and out of the entrance to the car park.

Mr Baker and Sergeant Parker looked bored and annoyed as she walked past them to the rear of the vehicle. She tried the silver key, which fit nicely with a jiggle. She opened the tall rear door, forcing her to take several steps backwards. She was joined by Mr Baker and Sergeant Parker.

Then it hit her—an odd, pungent smell—as she looked down at the body that lay resting on the sliding casket carrier.

Mr Baker noticed her scrunched-up facial expression and remarked, 'The smell of a corpse is foul, isn't it?'

'It's not my favourite smell,' remarked PC Cooper, trying to appear stoic after being embarrassed by the coroner.

'Right. I've seen enough to make me curious. We'll need to get her to the local pathologist for further examination. I'll set off now and call ahead so they know we're coming. We simply cannot leave the body here,' Mr Baker said, taking charge of the situation.

After a brief conversation, Mr Baker shared the address of the pathologist's office and detailed directions. PC Cooper attentively noted down the information. He turned and strode briskly towards his car, evidently eager to assist with the process.

Sergeant Parker nodded in agreement. 'Sounds like a plan. PC Cooper, can you accompany Mr Baker to the pathologist's office? You have the details, you can join him there,' he instructed, nodding towards Mr Baker. 'First, I'll need you to tell Mr Whitford we are holding him in custody. After you've done that, I need you to take the body to the coroner for a post-mortem examination.' Sergeant Parker turned to walk back to the entrance.

Keeley protested, 'You can't be serious? Shouldn't we ask them to collect it?'

Sergeant Parker paused. 'No, Keeley. We must ensure that the body isn't tampered with. While I'm not fully convinced that Mr Whitford is the culprit, we can't disregard his unusual theory that it wasn't a suicide. We wouldn't be doing our job if we dismissed every elderly person who cried wolf in this town. Moreover, the assistant coroner appears somewhat persuaded, so we're committed to following this path for now.'

'Alright, I'll handle Mr Whitford first, then take care of that,' Keeley said.

'One more thing, Keeley.'

'Yes, sir?'

'Try to obtain a copy of his military records, if there are actually any. I want to verify if he's being truthful.'

'Will do,' Keeley affirmed.

With her instructions clear, Keeley headed back into the station, where she briefed PC Seddon on the morning's events, explaining that Mr Whitford was suspected of murder.

'Another favour, Paul. Sarge wants us to try and obtain Mr Whitford's military records. They might shed some light on the situation,' she added.

PC Seddon nodded in acknowledgement as Keeley prepared to speak to Mr Whitford again.

'Understood, Keeley. I'll get right on it and see what I can find out about him,' he replied.

A sleepy Mr Whitford didn't seem too perturbed by Keeley's words. She left him nodding off at the table. Emerging from the station into the bright sunlight, Keeley's mind remained fixated on the unsettling discovery of the body and the enigmatic Mr Whitford. The morning's events replayed in her mind as she walked to the hearse.

Keeley sat in the hearse and adjusted the mirror. Her eyes were drawn to a faded photograph on the dashboard—a young Mr Whitford standing with his arm draped around the shoulder of another naval officer, both sharing hearty laughter. The identity of the other man in the photograph captured her interest.

After a deep breath, Keeley started the engine, her mind fixed on the journey ahead. The discovery of the body still weighed heavily on her thoughts, and the strange connection between Mr Whitford—an unassuming funeral director—and a potential murder, puzzled her. Questions crowded her mind as she drove towards the coroner's office. Did Mr Whitford or someone else truly murder Lizzie? She tightened her grip on the steering wheel, determined to find answers to the mystery.

<u>6</u>

The Rolls-Royce drove along White House Road in the morning sunlight.

Keeley gripped the wheel and focused on the road as the engine emitted a steady hum. She deftly navigated the winding route until she arrived at the imposing structure at the edge of the industrial estate.

Before stepping out, she stole a final glance at the body in the back—a solemn reminder of her purpose.

After a few minutes, she located the intercom panel beside the door and pressed the button labelled "Reception". A soft buzz filled the air, momentarily breaking the silence.

A voice crackled through the intercom. 'Hello, Ipswich Coroners Court...'

'Hi, this is PC Cooper. We spoke this morning. Mr Baker should be expecting me.'

Moments later, the front entrance opened, and

Mr Baker appeared with two men wearing gloves and pushing a gurney.

'PC Cooper, this is Dr Pilkington who will be helping us this morning,' said Mr Baker

'Morning officer,' said Dr Pilkington.

Keeley pointed to the Rolls-Royce hearse and they all walked over to it.

She stepped back as the boot swung open, revealing the body inside. She wrinkled her nose and held her breath.

'Not seen many dead bodies before, officer?' Dr Pilkington asked.

'Can you tell this is my first time?' Keely replied.

'It's obvious,' Dr Pilkington said. 'You'll get used to it.'

'I hope I don't have to!'.

They slid the body out and carefully moved it onto the gurney, tightening the surrounding straps around the upper body and then the ankles. After closing the rear of the hearse, they pushed the gurney into the entrance of the building.

The coroner's office was sparse and plain. A woman sat behind the reception desk, busily tapping away on her computer while speaking on the phone.

Dr Pilkington nodded in her direction. They navigated along the corridor, where he used his key card to unlock the door. He stepped into the room, ducking under the doorway. They each entered the examination room following his lead, where automated lights illuminated the room as they entered.

Keeley's eyes darted around the examination room, noting its sterile surroundings. In the centre stood a solitary silver autopsy table, its polished surface gleaming under the fluorescent lights.

Dr Pilkington and the other man pushed the gurney and transferred the body onto the autopsy table with care. The other man then left, and Dr Pilkington closed the door behind them.

Keeley examined the body on the table. Her stomach churned again and she fought against the rising bile, her throat tightening in revolt. She clenched her teeth.

Dr Pilkington walked over to a cupboard, where he removed three lab coats. He put one on himself, then removed his gloves and replaced them with a new pair. He grabbed another pair and thrust them, along with the lab coats, towards Keeley and Mr Baker.

'Put these on,' said Dr Pilkington

Keeley and Mr Baker took the lab coat and gloves from him.

Dr Pilkington cleared his throat, directing his words at Keeley. 'I've reviewed the post-mortem report for Miss Lizzie Hargrave, as provided by Mr Walsh. Her cause of death, according to the report, is drowning, specifically due to submersion in a liquid. In cases of acute drowning, it results in hypoxemia, which results in irreversible cerebral anoxia—'

'Hold on! What does that mean?' asked Keeley.

'Sorry, bad habit of mine. Essentially, removing the medical jargon, the body was starved of oxygen and some amount of the liquid was inhaled into the lungs,' he explained.

Keeley nodded, jotting down notes as he rambled on.

'From our examination, it seems that Miss Hargrave's cause of death was due to a lack of oxygen caused by being submerged in liquid, leading to irreversible brain damage.'

'Any signs of foul play?' Keeley asked.

'Let me check,' Dr Pilkington replied, reading from the report. 'That's odd, there is no report available. According to the notes on our system, the coroner's office was notified. They determined that although the death was unnatural, there was nothing suspicious to warrant a post-mortem examination.'

Keeley flicked through the pages of her police notebook, reviewing the notes she had taken during her earlier interview with Mr Whitford.

'Mr Whitford said he saw bruising under her armpits, like she was dragged.'

Dr Pilkington flicked through the pages of the report.

'The report doesn't show anything to confirm this. But since she's here, let's take a closer look.'

Dr Pilkington carefully lifted the woman's left

arm.

'Here we are. It's subtle, but it appears to be a muscle contusion under the left armpit. Let's check the other side,' he said, moving around the table to lift the woman's other arm and check for similar bruising.

'More prominent is the bruising on this side,' said Dr Pilkington, examining the area. 'Difficult to spot to the untrained eye.'

'I'm surprised Mr Fitzgerald did not include these findings in his report. Are we sure nothing else has been overlooked?' Mr Baker commented.

'So, Mr Whitford is right?' Keeley asked.

Mr Baker interjected, 'Let's not be so hasty in jumping to conclusions.'

'Determining the cause of death in such cases is often complex,' Dr Pilkington explained, carefully selecting his words. 'Drowning is frequently observed in bodies found in water, making it challenging to definitively identify it as the primary cause of death. A comprehensive analysis of all available evidence, including medical history, is essential for drawing accurate conclusions. Moreover, in this instance, the bruising on the body might have developed post-mortem, potentially resulting from manipulating the body after it had been submerged for a considerable duration. Water exposure can render the skin more susceptible to bruising.'

Keeley glanced at her notes, then looked up at

Dr Pilkington with a thoughtful expression.

'When Mr Whitford was preparing the body,' she began, 'he found it odd that the mouth was clamped shut, and there were no signs of external foam around the mouth—only in the nostrils. What do you think about that?'

'Interesting.' Dr Pilkington turned to the report, his eyes scanning rapidly, and his brow furrowing. 'Here we are. The report confirms the presence of foam in both nostrils, but there's no mention of the mouth,' he explained.

'If there's nothing in the report, could it have been missed? Can we take a quick look now?' Keeley enquired, her curiosity piqued.

'Unfortunately not, the passage of time and the multiple transfers have made it nearly impossible to ascertain the existence of foam around the mouth. The evidence has been compromised.'

Mr Baker turned to Dr Pilkington. 'Can we get a toxicology done?'

'Yes, but you should know that our testing process typically takes four to six weeks,' Dr Pilkington explained. 'I'll initiate the request now and keep you updated. I'm sorry if my answer doesn't match what you were hoping for. Based on our comprehensive examination, we haven't found any signs of suspicious physical trauma or cardiac conditions. The most likely conclusion is that drowning was the cause of her death. However, we can't determine definitively whether it was an accident or an intentional act of suicide.'

'Thank you for your time,' Keeley replied appreciatively. 'I'll be heading back to the station to report this.'

'Please store Miss Hargrave while we notify the family. In the meantime, I'll try to contact my boss to ask about the bruising and external foam and why they are missing from his report. Although we'll have to wait until he returns from his holiday in the Maldives,' said Mr Baker.

Keeley began to remove her lab coat and gloves, dropping them into the bin as she exited the room. She trailed behind Mr Baker, retracing their steps back to the desolate car park.

Conflicting emotions churned within her. She wanted to trust Mr Whitford, but doubts lingered. Sergeant Parker's advice echoed in her thoughts as she returned to the Rolls-Royce.

7

Driving back to the station, Keeley couldn't shake the nagging feeling that something was amiss. Mr Whitford's theories about foul play continued to echo in her mind. She hummed a tune under her breath, desperately trying to calm her racing thoughts and push the morning's unsettling events to the back of her mind.

As Keeley drove through the picturesque village of Wangford, the quaint cottages and lush greenery created a serene backdrop. The winding road, flanked by charming stone houses, evoked a sense of tranquillity.

Out of nowhere, an object hurtled towards Keeley, striking the windscreen with a deafening bang. Her heart raced as she clutched the steering wheel, desperately fighting to regain control.

As the Rolls-Royce veered off the road, Keeley

braced herself for impact. Instinctively, she shielded her head with her forearms just before the vehicle crashed into a hedge, jolting her forward into the steering wheel.

The collision caused a sharp pain and disorientation, unexpected since she'd never been in one before.

Feeling slightly dazed and shaken, Keeley initially struggled to move, her head throbbing from the impact. She tugged at the seatbelt, which refused to release; the jammed buckle trapped her in the aftermath of the collision. Drawing on her training, she carefully manoeuvred the seatbelt across her lap, painstakingly freeing one leg after another. With a determined yank in the opposite direction, she finally broke free from the confining grip of the seatbelt.

Looking around the interior, she spotted the faded photograph on the floor. She collected it and put it in her pocket. Exiting the vehicle, she climbed the sloping ditch and turned back to survey the scene with growing frustration.

'What the hell was that?' she muttered, her eyes scanning the immediate vicinity.

Keeley stared at the cracked windscreen, and it dawned on her. 'Must have been a seagull,' she concluded with a sigh.

A large crack marred the windscreen, and white feathers clung to the damaged area.

She scanned the surroundings, but the ill-fated bird was nowhere to be seen.

Keeley reached for her phone and tried to call for a recovery truck. Yet instead of the familiar ringing tone, her phone emitted an agitated, rapid series of beeps. She glanced at the home screen with a frown, only to find she had no signal in her current location.

With reluctant steps, she began walking back towards the small village she had passed earlier for help.

Following a brief walk, impatience overcame her. Retrieving her phone once more, she received two bars of signal. She dialled the number again and held her phone to her ear and hoped it would be enough signal to make the call.

The recovery company optimistically promised they would be with her in an hour. Reluctant to wait around for them to arrive, Keeley decided to call the station to request a ride back instead.

After what felt like a considerable wait, Keeley spotted a car approaching from the opposite side of the road. It bore the familiar yellow and blue Battenburg markings, slowing down before smoothly executing a turn and coming to a stop right in front of her.

Walking towards the passenger side, she saw her colleague, Sergeant Morgan. Since joining the team, Morgan has been like a mentor to Keeley, creating a strong camaraderie as the only other female colleague.

Opening the door, Keeley settled into the passenger seat, ready to get back to the station.

'Are you okay? What happened?' Sergeant Morgan asked, glancing out of the window at the Rolls-Royce before turning her piercing hazel eyes back towards Keeley. Her hand landed gently on Keeley's thigh, patting it.

Keeley's chest tightened, giving her a momentary urge to open up to Sergeant Morgan. Yet, memories of past heartbreak kept her quiet.

'Yeah...a seagull, of all things! It crashed into the windscreen,' Keeley replied, her voice quivering slightly.

Sergeant Morgan stifled a snicker. 'At least you're okay. More than we can say for the vehicle and the poor bird!' she said, almost laughing.

'It's not a joke, Hannah! Both Sergeant Parker and Mr Whitford won't be pleased,' Keeley said seriously.

Sergeant Morgan, sensing Keeley's frustration, turned to her with a concerned look. 'You know, Keeley, you don't always have to worry about what everyone thinks of you. Sergeant Parker may be tough, but he's not blind. He sees your talent, and he's hard on you because he cares. Plus, your mum being a big shot down in London just means the expectations are unfortunately high for you.'

Keeley glanced at her with surprise. 'You think so?'

'Absolutely. Stop fishing for compliments,

Keeley. Just keep doing what you do best, and don't let the pressure get to you. Now, as lovely as this place is, let's get back to the station.' She grinned as she flicked her indicator on and rejoined the road.

Keeley looked at the abandoned Rolls-Royce in the ditch, and a sigh escaped her lips. The morning had been a relentless cascade of bizarre events, pushing her to her limit.

8

The room had white tiles with sporadic, teal-patterned strips. There was one window, steel bars and frosted glass, offering a glimpse of the outside. He drummed his fingers as he sat on the room's only seat, a squeaky blue vinyl mattress, tired of standing.

His mind wandered to a pivotal encounter years ago in Lowestoft's town centre—a moment etched in his memory like a stubborn scar. Defending a group of girls against rowdy lads, Cecil's unwavering principles led him to speak up, intending to provide a measured critique. But things escalated quickly. Cecil, reacting in self-preservation, unexpectedly knocked the lad out. The incident was captured on video, leading to his arrest. The viral footage haunted him, a constant reminder of the complexities tied to his good intentions.

As a funeral director and former Navy

medic who had encountered countless bodies, something about Lizzie Hargrave's body unsettled him like never before. The memory of retrieving her motionless form from the hospital mortuary haunted him.

When Lizzie's sister, Lisa Bardwell, arrived to identify the body, grief consumed her, overwhelming her with guilt for not doing more to prevent Lizzie's suicide. In a desperate search for answers, she retraced their shared history, second-guessing her own actions and berating herself for missing subtle cues. As they arranged the funeral service at St Margaret's Church, her sorrow seemed mixed with restlessness.

Cecil's mind then drifted to the unsettling discovery of the previous night. Recounting the interview with Sergeant Parker and PC Cooper, he found himself reconsidering the evidence he had initially uncovered, realising its inherent weakness. Despite the absence of concrete evidence, the sister's candid revelations and the rarity of adult bath drownings left a gnawing doubt, whispering to him that someone might have orchestrated a carefully constructed deception.

After much deliberation, he dialled '1...0...1,' recounting his evening and the unsettling findings regarding Miss Hargrave's death. Scepticism tainted the responses on the other end. Cecil couldn't escape the burden of uncertainty, his fate hanging in the balance.

That's when he chose to act. Opting for the early morning to evade attention, urgency tinged his message, yet doubts lingered. Now he found himself trapped within the police station's walls, considered a potential suspect in a murder case he had no connection to. He couldn't help but acknowledge they were taking him quite seriously now.

Cecil strengthened his resolve. He had to uncover the truth and clear his name, even if it meant risking his unwavering principles in the pursuit of justice.

9

Pulling into the station's car park, Sergeant Morgan deftly manoeuvred her vehicle into the same parking space where Mr Whitford's hearse had been that morning.

Undoing her seatbelt, Keeley turned towards Sergeant Morgan. 'Hannah, I really appreciate you coming to pick me up.'

'No problem. You owe me a wine when we next go out,' Sergeant Morgan replied, leaning closer in her seat.

'Deal! You know I never need much of an excuse to enjoy an evening out with you,' Keeley said, a playful smile spreading across her face.

In the late afternoon sun, Keeley left the car park and returned to the police station.

Back at her desk, she prepared to catch up on paperwork and follow up on any pending cases. Her focus was broken by the ringing of her phone.

Swiftly answering, she said, 'How can I assist you?'

A rough-sounding man replied, 'Hey, it's Graham from Wangford Elite Motors. We've got your vehicle, love. The Rolls-Royce hearse with the cracked windscreen, is that yours?'

Keeley didn't want to get into explaining why it wasn't hers but felt it was her obligation to repair the damage. 'Yes, that's the one. Have you managed to fix it?'

'Nah, not yet. I've been searching high and low for a replacement. It's not easy to find parts for a car this old! I found a new windscreen online for £549. It's not cheap, but it's the only one I could find. You want me to order it?'

Keeley hesitated for a moment before conceding. 'Okay, go ahead and order it. I need to get the car back as soon as possible.' It was not ideal that such a chunk of her monthly pay would go towards repairing the damage. Damn bird!

After her call, Keeley noticed an unfamiliar brown folder on her desk. She proceeded to open the folder labelled "Lt Cdr Cecil Whitford Military Record."

With keen interest, she sat forward and began poring over its contents. She first skimmed the header at the top that read *Ministry of Defence*, then skipped past details she already knew about him.

As she scanned the page, her attention was

drawn to the character description section. The words on the page painted a clear picture of Lt. Cdr Whitford—a portrait of steadfast loyalty, sharp intelligence, a caring demeanour, a strong work ethic, an occasional touch of sarcasm, a wellspring of wisdom, unwavering bravery, bold audacity, and a strong sense of protectiveness. It was remarkable how, despite having only met him earlier that day, the words resonated so deeply, as if the text had brought his very essence to life on the page before her.

Turning to his service record, she read about how he had served aboard the HMS Frigate RELENTLESS and HMS LOWESTOFT; he had served aboard these ships during the Cold War Era. He had impressively reached the rank of Lieutenant Commander (Lt Cdr), a senior officer rank in the Royal Navy.

Further down the page, she read how his journey began at the age of eighteen when he enlisted as a medical officer. He underwent a rigorous ten-week basic training regimen at HMS RALEIGH, a shore base nestled in Torpoint, Cornwall, where he also successfully completed his swimming test. This initial phase was just the start. He then delved into a forty-week intensive professional training programme, honing his knowledge and technical skills to attain the competence of a medical assistant.

His learning journey extended across the country through various clinical placements.

Eventually, he returned to DMS Whittington, a period of consolidation paving the way for his graduation. With his newly acquired skills, Lt. Cdr Whitford embarked on his maiden assignment aboard the HMS SERAPHIM, his first ship.

But his quest for knowledge didn't cease there. A twelve-week stint at HMS COLLINGWOOD followed, dedicated to the Junior Officers' Leadership Course, a pivotal step in his growth as a naval officer.

From his service record, it appears that his first mission was part of the ongoing conflict with the Icelandic Coast Guard. It was known as the Cod Wars, and Royal Navy ships were involved in attempts to cut the nets of Icelandic trawlers. He served on this mission for over two and a half years and was promoted to lieutenant.

After six years had passed, he then served on HMS ARK ROYAL. Following this, he was promoted to Lieutenant Commander.

In the later years of his service, he was part of several other conflicts around the world.

She turned to the last page of the report, with honours and medical discharge in bold print.

On June 10, 1980, Lt Cdr Whitford was part of a UN aid mission in Peru after a devastating earthquake struck off the coast claiming approximately 70,000 lives. He played a crucial role in rescuing survivors, risking his life alongside his team in dangerous landslides, and saving children who had become trapped in a school bus.

As she read further, Keeley's respect for Mr Whitford only grew. She couldn't help but admire the man who had risked his own safety to save others.

According to the medical log, Lt. Cdr Whitford sustained a back injury when he fell down a mountain during a mission. This injury led to his medical discharge due to damage to his back muscles. In recognition of his bravery, he was awarded the Queen's Commendation for Bravery.

'Cooper! My office, now!' Sergeant Parker's command rang out urgently.

Keeley closed the report. She gripped it close to her chest, marching towards Sergeant Parker's office.

Sergeant Parker glanced up from his desk and asked, 'So, what's the update from the pathologist?'

Keeley recounted the details of her conversation with Dr Pilkington and Mr Baker, explaining their theories.

Sergeant Parker furrowed his brow, lost in thought, before replying, 'Okay, so we can determine Mr Whitford is not guilty of murder, and this is all a case of police time being wasted by an old man looking for adventure,' snarled Sergeant Parker.

Keeley slid the report across the desk towards Sergeant Parker.

'I agreed with that theory until I read this. Sir, I've gone through his military record. In a past life, he was a hero. Maybe he knows more than we think about these types of situations.'

Sergeant Parker lifted the report and casually flipped through its pages, his expression showing signs of scanning with feigned interest.

'Maybe we didn't fully grasp Mr Whitford's situation. But honestly, it's water under the bridge now. The coroner has already ruled it a suicide. Our focus needs to shift to other cases, and we can go ahead and let Mr Whitford go. On another note, I need you to make a call to Miss Hargrave's family. We should update them on what happened today. Just hold off on mentioning Mr Whitford's theory. They've already been through a lot, and there's no need to add this extra stress to their plate right now.'

Keeley spoke with Miss Hargrave's family, conveying essential details with empathy. She navigated the discussion skilfully, choosing to omit any reference to Mr Whitford's theory for the time being.

The family reacted negatively to the news that their funeral director had driven Miss Hargrave around town. Keeley found herself listening to threats of legal action against Mr Whitford and a potential formal complaint against the station. Despite the challenges, she managed to soothe their concerns to the extent that they attributed the incident to an elderly man's lapse in reality.

Though tempted, Keeley refrained from inserting the fact that Mr Whitford had their best interests at heart, understanding that their anger was currently clouding their judgement.

Continuing to read Mr Whitford's military record, she recognised its significance. With some determination, she made up her mind. Despite the coroner's ruling and Sergeant Parker's doubt, Keeley felt the case held hidden truths worth investigating further.

<u>10</u>

Keeley made her way down the hallway, her steps echoing softly in the dimly lit corridor, leading her to the custody suite where Mr Whitford was being held.

She unlocked the heavy door and entered the room, finding Mr Whitford seated on the edge of the bed. His bow tie had been removed and his jacket lay folded neatly beside him.

A wry smile danced across Mr Whitford's lips as he greeted her, 'PC Cooper, it's been some time since our paths crossed.'

'I'm sorry for the wait, Mr Whitford. I've just come back from the coroner's office.'

'Did they agree with my theory?'

'I'm sorry, Mr Whitford. The coroner wasn't convinced. While your findings were intriguing, they didn't establish foul play.'

'What happens next?' he asked, shrugging and studying Keeley intently.

'I told the family, and they're upset. They're looking for a new funeral director to pick up her body from the coroner's office and continue with the funeral.'

'I understand. Believe me, the last thing I wanted was to add more burden to the family at an already difficult time. Am I facing charges?'

'No, sir, on this occasion, Sergeant Parker has given you leniency on the basis that you did this with good intentions of reporting a crime, although the manner in which you did it was slightly unorthodox.'

'I appreciate it. May I have my keys and belongings so I can leave? My job isn't confined to regular hours. Death doesn't adhere to a schedule,' he remarked, smirking at Keeley.

Keeley smiled briefly but then looked concerned.

Mr Whitford's keen eyes caught the shift in Keeley's demeanour. 'What's on your mind, PC Cooper? You seem troubled,' he enquired with genuine concern.

'Well, when driving your vehicle back from the coroner's office, a bird cracked your windscreen,' Keeley replied hesitantly, trying to downplay the severity of the windscreen needing to be replaced as well. Keeley was surprised to hear Mr Whitford laughing uncontrollably.

'I'm sorry, Mr Whitford. I've arranged for repairs and will cover the cost. Should be ready in a few days,' Keeley assured. 'Is there someone you can call to pick you up? Perhaps your wife?'

Mr Whitford's laughter filled the room, though his expression turned pensive as he thought back to his ex-fiancée—a person he hadn't contemplated in quite some time. Retrieving his jacket from the bed, he responded.

Mr Whitford smiled softly. 'No, I'm not married. I'll just order a taxi home,' he said.

Keeley paused for a moment, 'Look,' she said, 'I feel bad about what happened to your car. How about I give you a ride home?'

Mr Whitford nodded.

'Okay then. Before we can go, I need you to complete some paperwork,' she said as she passed several forms to him.

'Keeley, Sarge wants to see you,' said PC Seddon from the corridor.

'Will be right there,' Keeley replied then turning back to Mr Whitford who was busily scanning and filling in the forms. 'I'll be right back.'

As she made her way to Sergeant Parker's office, she rapped on the closed door and heard his muffled reply, 'One moment...fine...Yes, come in.'

Keeley opened the door and stepped into the room, where she proceeded to inform Sergeant Parker about her conversation with Miss Hargrave's family.

'Alright, to prevent any further complications with the family and to safeguard the station's reputation, I need you to go to the funeral and ensure that Mr Whitford doesn't show up. The family has already been through a lot, and we don't want to add to their grief. Keeley, I'm relying on you for this.'

'Will do, sir.'

After speaking with Sergeant Parker, Keeley met Mr Whitford at the entrance. Still on duty, Keeley led him to her squad car.

Inside, Mr Whitford spoke first to break the silence, 'Officer, I have a feeling there's more to Miss Hargrave's death. Something still feels off.'

'What do you mean?'

'I'm not sure,' he said, shaking his head slightly. 'I'm worried this case isn't closed. Something is hidden, waiting to come to light. If your boss and the coroner don't think it's murder, we might find another body sooner than we expect.'

'I hope not, Mr Whitford.'

11

As they stopped at the lights, Cecil glanced at a nearby wall. They turned the corner onto Denmark Road and Katwijk Way.

'There used to be a large Banksy mural of a seagull on that wall back there,' said Mr Whitford as he pointed. 'I bet you're glad that the bird that crashed into you wasn't that big!'

Almost forgetting Mr Whitford's presence, she turned to him, a warm smile lighting up her face.

'Yeah, I know the one, I've driven past it countless times. It's a shame it's gone. And yes, your car would be a lot worse off!' Keeley responded with a hint of amusement in her voice. They shared a chuckle.

'Here's a naval tidbit for you. We call seagulls *Shitehawks*!' Mr Whitford quipped.

Keeley's eyebrows raised in mild surprise. 'I never knew that. Speaking of your time in the Navy,' Keeley began, 'I went through your military file earlier today. You've had an impressive career. You must be proud to have received the Queen's Commendation for Bravery. I looked it up earlier. Not many are honoured in such a way.'

He shrugged. 'I guess, but it didn't last long. These days, my injuries make walking tough. But I felt good helping those who needed it. Joining the Navy was like a calling. I wanted to make a difference and keep people safe.'

'That's something. My dad served too. He was part of the Royal Anglian Regiment in Northern Ireland.'

'Interesting. What made you want to join the police? Did you not fancy following in his footsteps?'

'I was tempted. I actually followed my mum. She is an officer with the Metropolitan Police.'

Fleeting memories of his own mother, who passed away from bowel cancer when he was young, came back to him. 'Impressive family! I'm certain she must be proud of your accomplishments.

'Well,' she hesitated before continuing, 'my mum never supported my choice to move to Lowestoft. She wanted me to follow her into the Metropolitan Police.'

'Maintaining family legacies is tough,' Mr Whitford acknowledged. 'Why didn't you follow in your mother's footsteps? What brought you to Lowestoft?'

Keeley shifted in her seat, considering her response. 'It's a good question. A mix of reasons, really. This place holds childhood memories, we used to come here for holidays. I also wanted to get away from home, start building a life somewhere familiar but away from the usual.' She shrugged. 'And, honestly, it's growing on me.'

Whitford nodded and smiled. 'It does have a certain quaint charm, doesn't it? It's the white brick building just up here on the right.'

Stopping the car, she read the illuminated sign on the building: "Whitford & Sons Ltd."

'I'm sorry today has been such an ordeal. I was certain that Miss Hargrave had been murdered. Maybe I'm losing it,' said Mr Whitford.

'Tomorrow's a new day, Mr Whitford. You had good intentions. Maybe next time, pop into the station without any bodies first,' replied Keeley.

Mr Whitford nodded and began to exit the vehicle.

'Can I ask about the Latin phrase on your key ring? I'm curious what it means.'

Mr Whitford glanced down at the key ring and smiled. 'Ah, that's the motto of the Royal Navy,' he said. 'It translates to 'If you seek peace, prepare for war.'

Keeley raised an eyebrow. 'Really?' she said, intrigued. 'That's interesting.'

Mr Whitford nodded. 'Yes, it is,' he said. 'From my time in the Royal Navy, it has been a motto that has always resonated with me. It's a reminder to always be prepared and vigilant, even in times of peace. Thank you for the lift. I must get going. Early start tomorrow.'

'It's truly the least I can do. And once again, I apologise about your car. I'll certainly keep you updated on the repairs. Here's my card in case you need anything or happen to stumble upon more suspicious cases,' she offered, handing her card to Mr Whitford. 'Oh, before I forget, I found this photograph in your car amidst the chaos. I didn't want it to go missing.' Keeley explained as she passed the photograph to him.

Mr Whitford paused, staring with great interest at the picture. 'Thank you. I appreciate it.'

'Someone special?'

'Something like that. An old friend from long ago. Story for another time.'

The cool evening air brushed against his skin as he headed for his front door, the scent of saltwater mingling with the distant, rhythmic crashing of waves. The day had unfolded in ways he hadn't anticipated, leaving him without a car and facing the stark truth that Miss Hargrave's body was no longer under his care.

The conversation with the young police officer about family legacies led him to reflect on his own life's journey. Despite the simplicity of his existence, he could have pursued a medical career after leaving the Navy, despite his injuries. However, his father's impending loss to lung cancer introduced a certain irony - a funeral director needing to be buried. Once again, he was asked to take up the family business, as his father had before him.

Watching his grandfather and father console grieving families and prepare the departed, he naturally developed a talent for the profession.

Remembering the day he received his acceptance letter from the Royal Navy, pride surged within him. The recognition was especially satisfying because of the tough selection process. Bursting with excitement, he recalled rushing downstairs to find his father deeply engrossed in his work—delicately embalming a body, a task that had become routine. The distinct aroma of pickles had become a familiar scent in their home.

His father, a diligent World War II veteran, had a penchant for formal attire on every occasion, especially bow ties—a preference his mother often disapproved of. Their relationship, though characterised by understated affection, was built on evenings spent playing cards, with bridge emerging as a favourite pastime.

Presenting the acceptance letter evoked unexpected sadness from his father, whose own experience of war and aspirations growing up were also deeply tied to the family's legacy of funeral directing. As the only child, Cecil bore the weighty duty of carrying on the family tradition.

Cecil, feeling the weight of responsibility and

the reluctance to embrace it, had started training the next day without his father's blessing. Years later, he returned home to bury his father, a struggle that pushed him to contemplate taking his own life. But pride in upholding the family legacy kept him going.

He removed his suit and hung it neatly in the wardrobe. The wardrobe held only two crisp white shirts and several subtly patterned bow ties. He believed they added elegance to his appearance. A stark contrast emerged between today's materialistic generations and his ethos, forged during years spent abroad, where possessions were pared down to essentials, remaining a silent testament to his character.

Before climbing into bed, he stared at the five medals on the wall—a vivid reminder of a life left behind. PC Cooper's words about duty and pride resonated in his mind, like a compass guiding his actions.

Memories of helping others filled his thoughts, caring for the wounded and the deceased. Painful cries still echoed, but he found solace in knowing he had made a difference during his Navy service.

Running the family funeral business gave him purpose and an opportunity to honour not only his ancestors but also the values instilled in him throughout his journey.

As he lay there, looking at the ceiling, his thoughts wandered through the labyrinth of memories. With a contented sigh, he surrendered to the embrace of sleep, weary from the weight of the day but carrying the warmth of pride and purpose in his heart.

12

Cecil strolled along the beachfront, relishing the early morning breeze and the rhythmic symphony of waves. He sought solace in this familiar routine, attempting to unravel the mystery surrounding Lizzie Hargrave's death.

As he walked, he noticed a group of swimmers in sleek wetsuits glistening in the morning light, evoking memories of his Navy training days.

Back then, the ocean's bone-chilling embrace was a relentless adversary. Cecil could still hear the stern instructor's commands echoing in his mind, a constant reminder of his own perceived inadequacy; yet, with unwavering determination, he had faced those challenges head-on, overcoming his swimming limitations stroke by stroke.

His steadfast shipmate, Nigel, had stood beside him as a pillar of support through the countless failed attempts. Each setback only fuelled their shared resolve.

Amid frustrations and moments of doubt, Cecil and Nigel emerged victorious, passing the gruelling swimming test. Nigel's penchant for timing his laps culminated in an unexpected gift: a pocket watch. This watch became a symbol of their tenacity and a silent tribute to their unbreakable bond. Each setback only fuelled their shared resolve.

As the swimmers emerged from the water, Cecil's focus shifted from the past to the present. He retraced his steps, grains of sand clinging to his shoes. He remembered the days of his youth —the narrow alleys, fondly named 'The Scores,' were his childhood haven. He and his friends had imagined grand adventures, seeing themselves as intrepid sailors exploring uncharted waters.

A vivid memory resurfaced—his father's voice guiding him through bustling docks, marvelling at fishing boats laden with ocean treasures. The waterfront had left an indelible mark on Cecil, nurturing his lifelong devotion to the sea and its history.

Cecil passed old houses, worn cobblestone streets, and gas lamps casting a nostalgic glow. He smiled to himself as he acknowledged how the past and present merged.

His journey led him to a narrow passage, a childhood haven he had dubbed his 'secret hideout.' A slender alleyway nestled between two buildings had been his refuge, a place of solitude where he could look out upon the distant sea and dream of adventures beyond the horizon. These alleys had not only been his playground but also the forge that had shaped his unwavering passion for maritime exploits—a passion that ultimately led him to the Royal Navy.

As he clutched the pocket watch in the palm of his hand, a token of triumph, his eyes returned to the swimmers. Each stroke of their determined journey mirrored his own path, a testament to overcoming challenges.

Renewed determination surged through him. He was determined to solve Lizzie's death, to unravel the mystery. Cecil embraced the urgency that had been missing, ready to confront the obstacles ahead, much like he had countless times before—for his country and himself.

13

The helicopter blades whirred loudly, making it hard for Cecil to hear anything else as he surveyed the ruined landscape of Ancash, Peru. The earthquake had torn through the region, leaving destruction in its wake, with sinkholes covering the roads and parked cars shaking on the trembling ground.

'Over there!' a medic shouted, grabbing Cecil's shoulder and urgently pointing to a cliff. Following the gesture, he saw a school bus teetering on the edge, pushed down by a massive landslide. The bus looked vastly different from the ones he knew back home, worn and neglected after years.

'This rescue's gonna be a tough one. Those landslides are ripping through the valley.'

'Yeah, they're a real headache!' someone shouted above the deafening roar of the helicopter's blades as it hovered over the earthquake-ravaged landscape.

Taking charge, Cecil's voice held authority as he gave directions. 'All right, listen up! We'll rappel down from this side of the helicopter. Two lines, one on each side. We have to get those kids out fast but carefully. Time is of the essence, lads. Let's move!'

The five-person crew nodded in agreement and sprang into action, using ropes to descend the chopper's side.

Cecil checked his harness, held the rope with a gloved hand, and prepared for the heart-pounding leap. A leap of faith, just like he'd done many times before.

Reaching the back door of the bus, Cecil peered inside. He saw fear on the young faces of the schoolchildren. His eyes were fixed on the broken back window. Quickly and urgently, he reached in and unlocked the door.

'Hola!' he said, extending his hand. 'Rapido!'

A hesitant child took his hand, a mix of fear and trust in their grip. One by one, the others followed, guided by Cecil. It was like a well-rehearsed rescue dance, getting them out of the bus and onto the waiting helicopter safely.

Despite his efforts, one child, a Peruvian girl around seven, remained trapped. Fear held her frozen. Cecil, determined, tried to climb into the bus. But the unstable cliff gave way, sending him crashing into the rocks. Pain and numbness surged through his back. He fought the discomfort and rescued the Peruvian girl before the bus plunged off the cliff.

Memories afterwards were hazy, a mix of awareness and unconsciousness. He vaguely remembered being carried on a stretcher and airlifted to Cerro de Pasco. Eventually, he woke up in a hospital bed, feeling the effects of the intense rescue mission.

Scenes around him were etched in his consciousness: stretchers and doctors frantically hopping around hallways, treating the injured. He recalled trying to understand the doctor, who was speaking in broken English and explaining his surgery—a cervical discectomy and fusion.

Abruptly jolted awake, the haunting memories of Peru surged back, a cascade of recollections that served as poignant reminders of that single day's profound impact on his existence.

Glancing at his pocket watch, he felt the persistent ache in his back.

In the kitchen, he poured himself a glass of milk and took two capsules of tramadol, mindful of the risk of dependency from past experiences with fellow soldiers.

As a funeral director, his days were a steady rhythm of guiding souls. Committed to his role, he sacrificed personal time for others, finding comfort in his dedication.

Following his precise morning routine, Cecil tackled unanswered messages. He reviewed and quickly responded to families, arranging meetings. The previous days had been chaotic, and his vehicle, Angel, had been unavailable. PC Cooper had returned it, apologising once more.

The rest of the morning was spent managing messages from the hospital and nursing homes. However, a determination surged through him today. Cecil found himself making an unusual decision—to attend a funeral uninvited.

14

In the days that followed on duty, Keeley found herself with fewer significant incidents to handle. Even though she was relieved that Mr Whitford hadn't returned with another body, an undeniable craving for more excitement remained within her. While relative calm prevailed, she couldn't help but yearn for a more exhilarating pace in her line of work.

Her mother's captivating stories from her time in the Met Police, filled with tales of tackling fraud, battling drug rings, and navigating high-stakes crimes, had deeply fuelled Keeley's fascination, intensifying her desire for thrilling and adrenaline-pumping experiences.

The funeral for Miss Hargrave was scheduled for the afternoon at St. Margaret's Church. Following Sergeant Parker's orders, Keeley had been tasked with attending.

She arrived early at her desk to get ahead of

her workload before having to make her way to the ceremony.

She sighed inwardly, not particularly excited about this assignment. Funerals, she thought, are never easy, especially when you're ordered to be there.

Keeley's phone began to ring.

'Hello, this is PC Cooper speaking. May I ask who's on the line?'

'It's Dr Pilkington. Do you remember me from when the old duffer brought that body to your station?'

'Yes, I do. What can I help you with today, Dr Pilkington?'

'Well, I have some good news for you—' There was a note of cautious enthusiasm in Dr Pilkington's voice.

'What is it?' Keeley interrupted. 'Did your boss agree with Mr Whitford's suspicions?'

'No, not that. I've been trying to reach him but I keep getting his voicemail which is rather annoying. However, we did manage to get the toxicology report back in record time. I was expecting to wait for several weeks at least.'

'And? What were the findings?'

Dr Pilkington hesitated before answering, 'Let me see. It shows her alcohol intoxication was elevated to 0.20 gr/%. But that might be a false positive due to post-mortem fermentation. There are no other reported chemicals, toxins, or poisons. It looks like we can rule out the possibility of her being dragged unconscious into the bath. If she was awake while being dragged, there would be physical signs.'

'I guess that rules out one possibility, at least. Thanks for staying on top of this, Dr Pilkington.'

Ending the call, Keeley glanced at the clock and realised she was running late for the funeral. With little time to spare, she rushed to the changing room, eager to shed her uniform in favour of sombre funeral attire.

Keeley stepped out of the station and climbed into her Fiat 500, the rain began beating against the car like a car wash. She set her sat nav for St. Margaret's Church, aiming to navigate the rain-soaked roads quickly.

Arriving, she parked her car and hurried towards the church. Time was running out. As she arrived, the church doors closed. She hoped that Mr Whitford hadn't managed to slip inside before her. The rain soaked her, causing her hair to tangle and her clothes to cling uncomfortably.

Keeley stood outside the entrance under her umbrella, trying to shield herself from the rain for an hour. The sombre tolling of church bells filled the air, creating a poignant atmosphere as the church doors finally swung open.

As mourners began to exit the church, Keeley surveyed the crowd as she scanned for the recognisable figure of Mr Whitford.

Her attention shifted to a group near the church's entrance. Amidst the now-dissipating crowd, this smaller gathering clung to each other, their hushed conversations mere whispers on the air.

In the midst of the dispersing mourners, Keeley's eyes locked onto a lone male figure dressed smartly. Although his face remained hidden beneath a lowered umbrella, she could sense the air of familiarity about him. Her focus sharpened as he exited the church, but a sudden burst of high-pitched shouting seized her attention, instantly jolting her senses into overdrive.

'How dare you show your face here! Get away from me!' a woman shouted at the man.

Much to her dismay, the exact situation she had sought to prevent unfolded right before her eyes—Mr Whitford had made an appearance.

15

Keeley swore under her breath as she sprinted towards the entranceway, her coat billowing behind her like a cape in the wind. Her instincts as a police officer kicked in, pushing her to intervene and restore order.

With determined strides, she closed the distance; each step sent water squelching beneath her shoes. Near the front, she spotted two men squaring up against each other; she hoped Mr Whitford had not caused offence. She knew he meant well.

As she approached, Keeley saw a tall man gripping Mr Whitford's lapels and shouting. The heated exchange of words became clearer as she got closer.

'You shouldn't have come here! That was a big mistake,' he yelled furiously.

'James! Leave him alone. He's not worth it. James get off him now! You're hurting him!' a sobbing woman cried out.

Keeley acted quickly, breaking through the crowd. She assessed the aggressor, who must be James. Then she observed the other man.

A wave of confusion washed over her as she realised it was not Mr Whitford. Keeley's mind raced, trying to piece together the unfolding situation.

Suddenly, the unknown man launched a wild haymaker, landing a powerful blow. Caught off guard, James stumbled backwards. Seizing the opportunity, the assailant swiftly retreated into the distance.

All eyes turned towards Keeley, as she emerged into the middle of the chaotic scene.

'Who are you?' the tearful woman asked.

Keeley's eyes flitted between the faces, gauging the tension, before she responded with a steady and professional tone, 'I'm PC Cooper, here at the family's request.'

The man got to his feet, dabbing at a cut lip with a handkerchief, his words edged with frustration. 'Well, if you're a police officer, you should've arrested the bastard who sucker punched me!'

'James, please! It's my sister's funeral!'

He nodded, glancing at the weeping woman.

'Thank you, officer. We spoke yesterday. The man bleeding over there, that's my husband, James.' Lisa steadied herself before continuing, 'I apologise for the ruckus. We appreciate your presence today.'

'I'm truly sorry for your loss. If it's not too difficult, may I ask for the name of the man who ran just now? I'd like to understand more about the situation,' Keeley asked.

'Oh, him,' Lisa began, her voice heavy with disdain. 'That would be Rob Hoskins, Lizzie's ex-boyfriend. A real piece of work. He's no doubt responsible for what happened to her!'

James approached them, he pulled his trench coat tighter attempting to shield himself from the rain. Then, he wrapped his arm around Lisa and drew her close.

'We best be heading to the wake. Come along, dear,' James said as he ushered Lisa away.

They and the remaining group headed off down the pathway towards St. Margaret's Road, where they had parked their vehicles.

The rain had thoroughly drenched Keeley as she also headed back down the pathway to her car, glad that Mr Whitford had not appeared; he would have only made things worse for the family today.

As she replayed the events of the funeral in her mind, the image of Lizzie's ex-boyfriend, Rob, stayed, his potential connection to Lizzie's mysterious situation weighing on her thoughts. Keeley felt a determination to dig into Rob's background, seeking answers and potential clues.

<u>16</u>

The rain drummed steadily on the car's windscreen, echoing Keeley's growing suspicion of deeper issues from the funeral altercation.

The memory of Sergeant Parker's directive remained, a suggestion, perhaps, that he didn't fully trust her instincts. 'What should I do?' Keeley mumbled to herself, then decisively dialled PC Seddon's number.

'Hey, Paul, it's Keeley. I need your help.'

'Sure, what's up?'

'I need a background check on a name.'

'What's the name?'

'Mr Rob Hoskins. Robert, I assume.'

'Okay,' Paul replied, typing away. 'Here we go. Two results for that name.'

Keeley went on to describe the man who had punched the sister's husband at the funeral.

'Mr Robert William Hoskins, age 37. Lives at 8 Arnold Street. Is there anything else you need to know?'

'Thanks. One more thing. Could you also just check his arrest and recent incident records.'

'No problem. Let's see... two years in HMP Norwich for bodily harm. Some disturbance complaints, but nothing recent.'

Paul's words only deepened Keeley's concern, reinforcing her determination.

After ending the call, a realisation struck Keeley. The pieces of the puzzle were coming together: the troubled past, the violent ex-boyfriend – it all aligned with Mr Whitford's suspicions.

Despite Parker's request to drop the matter, Keeley couldn't ignore her instincts. What Lisa said and the urgency of the situation thrust her into action.

She hit the road, determined to uncover the truth.

17

Keeley pulled her car into the only available parking space outside 8 Arnold Street, taking a moment to survey the street and the house.

The rain had ceased its downpour, leaving her skin damp as she left her car—a welcome relief after the drenched journey she had endured.

Exiting her car, Keeley headed towards the front door of the greyish-blue-painted terrace house.

The iron gate creaked open as she approached the front door. She knocked a couple of times.

She knocked again, harder this time. Still no response. With an exasperated huff, she kicked the door lightly, letting out a muttered 'Come on.'

As she turned to head back to her car, she locked eyes with the man from the funeral. He stood there in his soaked black suit. Before she could react, he spun around and dashed away.

'Wait! Mr Hoskins, stop! Police—' Keeley's

command was cut short and her words hung in the air.

Keeley sprinted forward, resolute in her pursuit. Questions raced through her mind. Why would he flee? The question forced her on, in pursuit. Her breaths came in rapid gasps, her feet pounding against the pavement as she chased after Rob.

His pace began to pick up as he neared a local park. He clambered through bushes and climbed over a waist-high gate.

Keeley pursued him through the park, closely on his heels. Her dress didn't slow her down as she leaped over the gate. Her years of cross-country experience kicked in, yet her legs began to burn as she hurdled fallen tree branches and navigated the bushy maze as she ran.

She noticed him up ahead, stealing a nervous glance over his shoulder. She quickened her pace, closing the distance. The screech of tyres filled the air as the collision unfolded. Rob was thrown onto the car's bonnet, and then tumbled to the ground, dazed and shaken. He clutched his hip in pain, struggling to get back up. His eyes met Keeley's briefly, before he staggered to resume his escape, moving slower and more laboured now.

As Keeley passed the stopped car, the driver was inspecting his vehicle while cursing in Rob's direction, who had distanced himself. She continued to follow him down Raglan Street, noticing the dead-end sign ahead and quickened her pace in pursuit.

As she came around the corner she saw him in the distance. 'Stop, Rob!' she demanded.

Rob came to an abrupt stop, panting heavily and wiping the beads of sweat from his forehead with his sleeve. Panic filled his darting eyes as he realised he was trapped.

Keeley's plea echoed once more, 'I need you to stop immediately! I need to talk to you.' As she studied him, he appeared dishevelled, reminiscent of a train commuter racing for the last ride home.

Ignoring her, his eyes darted around, searching frantically for an escape route.

Keeley watched as a delivery van approached down the road, the driver seemingly distracted by packages on the dashboard. Suddenly, the driver abandoned the van, rushing toward a nearby property and leaving the engine running with the door ajar.

Keeley's eyes shifted between the yellow delivery van and Rob, who was watching her intently while also glancing towards the van.

Before she could react, Rob sprinted towards the vehicle.

'No, stop!' she cried as she desperately sprinted towards the delivery van.

The door slammed shut. She slammed her fist against the window, yelling in frustration, 'Open the door, Rob!'

In a tense moment of eye contact, Rob taunted her with a smirk. Then, with a swift motion, he shifted the gear stick into first, revved the engine, and sped off.

As the van retreated up the road, the delivery driver rushed to the curb, his hands raised in disbelief and anger. He unleashed a string of curses, realising his vehicle had been commandeered.

Keeley swiftly reached for her phone and dialled the station, her voice breathless as she relayed the situation. 'Hi, it's PC Cooper Can you put out a BOLO for a Caucasian male, approximately 37 years old? We need to question him regarding Miss Hargrave's case. He's around 5'9 with brunette hair. The suspect's name is Robert Hoskins. He was last seen wearing a black suit, and a white shirt. He fled in a delivery van with the licence plate numbers "Y-A-6-8-N-Y-C." I'm going to need another address also.'

18

The next day, Keeley headed down the private road, turning into the long driveway. The house was set back, hidden behind trees and hedging. She parked her car in front of one of the detached garages, alongside an expensive-looking white SUV, which was charging.

The gravel path crunched under her shoes as she approached.

A silhouette emerged behind the frosted glass of the door, furrowed brows revealing momentary concern.

'Hello again, Mrs Bardwell. It's me, PC Cooper. We met at your sister's funeral. I'm sorry for any alarm turning up unannounced like this.'

'...Oh, yes! Sorry, you startled me for a moment. Seeing the police at your front door is always cause for concern. Is everything okay?'

'I was hoping to ask you a few questions about your sister and Rob Hoskins. Would it be okay if I came in?'

Mrs Bardwell hesitated, 'Now's not really a good time.'

'Are you sure? It won't take long, just a few questions and I'll be on my way.'

Mrs Bardwell replied, 'Um, well... Okay, come on in.'

Keeley entered the Bardwells' spacious, tastefully decorated home. As she followed her through a corridor adorned with art, they reached a roomy kitchen breakfast area that opened into a garden room. The opulence of the surroundings struck Keeley, making her briefly reflect on the differences between her own modest home and this grandeur.

Mrs Bardwell slumped onto the kitchen island, her elbows pressing into the cool marble countertop. As Keeley inspected the scene, she couldn't help but notice a few subtle details. A half-empty glass of wine stood nearby, and beside it, an almost empty brown bottle of pills with a label marked 'FOR PROFESSIONAL USE ONLY.'

Keeley's eyes locked on the bottle, her brows furrowing slightly.

Mrs Bardwell hastily grabbed the bottle and put it in her pocket. 'Just to help me sleep,' she said, her smile tight and forced.

Keeley observed Mrs Bardwell, her strawberry-blonde hair cascaded untamed, and her eyes were puffy. The woman standing before her was notably different from the composed individual she had encountered at the funeral.

'I understand this is a challenging time, Mrs Bardwell. I'm here to ask you some questions about your sister, Lizzie, and her ex-boyfriend, Rob Hoskins, to aid our investigation.'

'Sure, go ahead. And call me Lisa,' she replied, her voice quivering.

'Thank you. Could you start by telling me about what Lizzie was like?'

'Well... um... Let me think. Lizzie was a warm-hearted and sociable person, passionate about her job as a science teacher. She always wore a smile and dreamed of starting a family someday. Kind and ever-willing to help others, perhaps too much. I might have been a bit hard on her being the older sister.' Lisa wiped away a tear that trickled down her cheek. 'I'm sorry. It's just...' Lisa's voice trembled, and tears welled in her eyes. She struggled to compose herself.

'I understand. I apologise for bringing up such a sensitive topic, but did Lizzie exhibit any signs of contemplating suicide?'

'No, not at all. To my knowledge, she was moving forward in life. However, she faced challenges in her relationship with Rob, especially during the lockdown due to the pandemic.'

'How so?'

'When the pandemic hit, he was furloughed and eventually lost his job. That created financial strain for them. Lizzie tried to remain strong around me, but I could sense the pressure they faced relying on a single income. As Rob struggled to find a new job, He started drinking during the day and often directed his frustration towards Lizzie, blaming her for their situation.'

'I'm sorry to ask, but did Rob ever become physically violent towards your sister?'

Lisa's eyes briefly shifted away before she confessed, 'I can't say for certain. Lizzie never mentioned anything to me. But I couldn't shake the feeling that he might have been abusive. I once saw some bruising on her wrist, but she dismissed it as an accidental injury. Then, a month later, she left him. I never liked Rob from the start, but I don't think he is entirely to blame.'

'Can you tell me more about that bruising on Lizzie's wrist?' Keeley asked.

Lisa continued, 'I think he had a troubled upbringing. I don't know much, but Lizzie told me a bit. He had some legal trouble in the past due to his abusive stepfather, who would use his mother as a punching bag from time to time. Must have been rough growing up.'

'Can you think of anything that might have happened recently that might suggest Lizzie was going through a tough time?'

Lisa hesitated, her eyes briefly shifting away. 'She constantly asked me for money, worried about her finances and the cost of living,' she admitted between sobs. 'I tried my best, but I couldn't keep giving her money with no strings attached.'

'How often did she ask you for money?'

'All the time. Money was a source of tension all the time, but I cared about her well-being, as she wasn't great at managing money. Our parents left us a modest inheritance when they passed away when we were young. She squandered it, while I invested mine. She often asked me for money back then, and I did my best to help her. I never expected things to turn out like this,' she said, tears in her eyes.

'I understand that Lizzie was under a lot of financial stress, and you did your best to help her. Did these financial issues cause any tensions between you two?'

'You see. Lizzie would beg for money. It wasn't just occasional help. It was relentless. She seemed to have no regard for the impact it had on me. At first, I was willing to assist my sister in her time of need, as family should. But it went beyond that. Lizzie's requests became more frequent and increasingly extravagant.'

Lisa's eyes welled up with tears, and her voice trembled as she continued.

'I liquidated some of my investments and bought her a house when she left Rob, she had nothing to her name when they separated.' She paused to collect herself. 'A few months later she came back to ask for more. I couldn't afford to keep giving her money, especially when she showed no restraint or gratitude. Lizzie's constant requests had led to a considerable strain on our relationship.'

Keeley proceeded with her inquiries, noting how Lisa's unease seemed to deepen as the conversation unfolded. The atmosphere seemed charged with an underlying tension, and Lisa's responses became more hesitant and guarded.

The front door slammed shut, capturing their attention.

A man's voice called out, 'Only me. I've just come to fetch some clothes. I'm out with colleagues after work later. Why is there a police car on the drive?'

Lisa began wiping away her tears with the arm of her jumper before calling out, 'I'm in the kitchen, love.'

The man from the funeral entered. Keeley stood tall.

'It belongs to PC Cooper. Remember her from Lizzie's funeral, dear?'

His piercing blue eyes briefly studied Keeley before nodding in acknowledgement.

'Yes. Hello again, officer. What can we help you with today?'

'I just had a few follow-up questions about Lizzie's death and about Rob,' Keeley explained.

He drummed his fingers on the countertop, 'Is this necessary? We've already given statements to the police,' James said.

'I'm sorry, Mr Bardwell. Following Mr

Hoskins's actions at the funeral, we needed to understand more about Lizzie and her relationship with Rob.'

'Why are you asking these questions? It was a suicide, wasn't it?' James questioned.

'Yes, it was, but we need to be thorough in our investigation,' Keeley responded.

Lisa's sobbing intensified, the heart-wrenching sound echoing through the room. James cast a concerned glance at her.

'Thank you for your time, PC Cooper,' he managed. He cast a concerned look toward Lisa, who continued to sob uncontrollably. 'My wife is going through a tough time,' he said, his hand extending gently to offer her solace. 'It might be best if you leave us be.'

'I just had a few more questions, if you don't mind?'

James clenched his fists, his knuckles white. 'We've given our statements already. As for Rob...' His voice grew sharper, 'He's a worthless individual who was never worthy of Lizzie. We hope to never see him again.'

Keeley's fingers tightened around her notepad, snapping it shut with a decisive flick. She forced a tight-lipped smile at Mrs Bardwell, her steps brisk as she retreated to her car.

Driving back to Lowestoft, she pulled over and began dialling a number on her phone.

'Any luck on Hoskins and the missing van?' asked Keeley.

'No luck, but I'll keep you updated if we find him.'

'Thanks, Paul. I need to find him, he is crucial to me unravelling the mystery of this case I'm working on.'

Hanging up the call, she continued her journey, letting out a heavy sigh.

19

In her dimly lit maisonette on Marine Parade, Lizzie poured another glass of wine after her guest's departure.

Hearing the brass knocker, she wondered who could visit at this late hour.

Opening the door, she was surprised to see her guest return.

'Why are you back? Have you forgotten something? We've already discussed this,' Lizzie asked while cracking the door open to let them in.

Lizzie walked to the table, sipping her wine and absentmindedly flipping through TV channels.

'You left me no choice.'

Suddenly, a gloved hand clamped over her nose and mouth, a noxious cloth pressed against her face. Panic surged through her, her instincts fighting against the unexpected attack.

The acrid smell of the substance on the cloth made her head spin. She could feel her body betraying her, growing weaker by the second. A fight she knew she couldn't win; the room blurred as the cloth took effect, pulling her into the suffocating depths of unconsciousness.

She was dragged up the stairs, the worn steps creaking. Each thud of her legs felt like a brutal reminder of her helplessness.

Near the top of the stairs, she heard the faint sound of water, distant and ominous, deepening her dread as she slipped back into unconsciousness.

The cold tiled floor stirred her back to semi-consciousness. She realised she was in the bathroom, the steady rush of water into the bathtub a disturbing soundtrack.

She watched the guest's silhouette moving, and then the bathroom door slammed shut.

Struggling to keep her eyes open, her speech slurred and desperate, she managed to choke out, 'But why... why?'

Her clothes were ripped from her body; trembling hands fumbled with buttons and sleeves until she lay bare on the bathroom floor.

A sudden jolt in her arm startled her, her eyelids growing heavier as she was lifted and lowered into the tub.

Fighting to stay awake, her strength slipping, the last thing she felt was her body sinking into the dark water.

20

'Stop,' she groaned, her voice tired. 'Enough.'

Groggily, Keeley fumbled for her phone, annoyed by its incessant buzzing.

It persisted, vibrating relentlessly on the bedside table, forcing her to sit up, grunting in frustration. She silenced it with a weary swipe of her finger.

Rubbing her eyes and stretching to ease her body, she climbed out of bed.

She reflected on the frustrating past few days. Firstly the visit to Mrs Bardwell left her feeling particularly uneasy about her admission that her sister was constantly bleeding her dry of money. Then she arrived at work the following day, to discover that the Assistant Coroner Mr Baker had lodged a complaint. Sergeant Parker was furious, even more so as it had embarrassed his leadership with the coroner's office, especially since the coroner's office had not opened an official investigation.

Everyone, Parker included, believed Miss Hargrave's death was a clear suicide.

She felt relieved to be off duty for a few days. The argument with Sergeant Parker made her want to seek solace on her couch while binge-watching TV and indulging in junk food over the next few days.

Ever since Mr Whitford turned up with that body, her life has been filled with inconvenience and unwelcome distractions. The complaint, aside from tarnishing her otherwise impeccable career path, bore the additional burden of demanding her to make amends with the family. A weight she couldn't afford. A looming blemish now menaced her painstakingly upheld record.

Her phone lit up and vibrated, it was her mother calling.

Weeks had passed since their last exchange and the idea of speaking to her now filled Keeley with a sense of unease. The echo of her mother's voice endured in her mind – 'When are you going to do real police work, Keeley?' The tone had etched itself into her memory.

She let out a heavy sigh, silencing the phone once again and dropping it on the sofa.

Maybe tomorrow, when she feels emotionally prepared, she would summon the courage to speak with her or maybe she would decide not to call at all. After all, her mother hadn't exactly made an effort to visit her since she moved to

Lowestoft.

She walked to the window and looked at the quiet street below. Lost in her thoughts, she jumped as her phone vibrated on the sofa.

She hesitated, uncertain about answering.

'Why not,' she blurted, grabbing it.

'Hi, Mother—'

'Keeley, is that you?'

Keeley panicked hearing a male voice, she looked down at her phone to realise it was work calling.

'Hello?'

'Keeley, it's Paul.'

'Paul, sorry thought you were my mother.'

'All good. I'm really sorry to be calling you on your day off, but we've tracked down Hoskins.'

'Excellent, where is he?

'He's checked into the Blue Harbour Hotel for two nights. Seeing as you logged the BOLO, we need you to come to the station to question him. Is he still a person of interest?'

She felt a knot tighten in her stomach, caught between the pursuit of justice and the chilling worry of potential repercussions.

'Keeley, are you there? What do you want me to do?'

'Yes. I'm on my way,' she replied.

She ended the call and quickly got ready.

21

Keeley arrived at the station and saw PC Seddon and Sergeant Morgan at their desks.

Sergeant Morgan's voice could be heard lecturing someone on the phone. They exchanged a playful gesture, her mimicking a gun to her temple.

Keeley continued towards PC Seddon, who was diligently typing away on his computer.

'Morning, Paul. Any luck with Hoskins?'

'Yes, got him! We've not long been back. Picked him up not long after we spoke. It was effortless, he was sound asleep and the front desk let us in. Hannah and I got an eyeful when he tried to flee down the hallway with no clothes on. Hannah only went and wrestled him to the ground. It was proper funny.'

'Good work. Sorry I missed it,' Keeley said, with a wry smile.

'He's all ready for you in room 2.'

Finishing up her conversation with PC Seddon, she headed over to Sergeant Morgan, who had just finished her call.

'It sounds like you've had an eventful morning.'

Sergeant Morgan looked sheepish and replied, 'More action than I've had in a while. He was quite well endowed.'

Keeley couldn't help but snigger, her shoulders shaking with amusement. 'Oh, Hannah, you're always so crude! What are you like?'

'Oh, I forgot Keeley Cooper is such a prude! Anyway, I guess you need a senior officer to interview him with you? Shall I do the honours? He might like seeing me again,' Sergeant Morgan suggested.

'Would you? That would be great,' Keeley agreed.

She headed to the changing rooms to switch into her uniform, then made her way to meeting room 2 where Sergeant Morgan was waiting outside the door.

Keeley entered first, followed by Sergeant Morgan. Sitting across the table was Rob Hoskins, she stared at the same man who she had chased around the town until he escaped in a delivery van.

Surprise flickered across his face and he quickly slumped his head into his hands, resting his elbows on the interview table. Next to him sat a plump man in a dark navy pinstriped suit and thick-rimmed glasses—the unmistakable appearance of his lawyer.

'Hello again, Mr Hoskins. I'm PC Cooper, you never gave me much of a chance to introduce myself the other day when I chased you around town. No doubt, you remember Sergeant Morgan from earlier? She remembers you,' Keeley said.

'It's nice to see you with your clothes on,' Sergeant Morgan added with a smile.

Keeley turned on the tape recorder and they all took their seats. She cautioned Rob for theft of a motor vehicle and went through his rights, which he agreed to. The interview started with the customary confirmation of the interview location, date, and time.

'Can you start by explaining why you decided to flee and steal a delivery van to escape when I came to your house the other day?'

'I didn't know who you were. I remembered seeing you briefly at the funeral and thought you were one of Lizzie's friends coming to pick a fight,' Rob replied.

'But why run? What were you scared of?' Keeley probed further.

'You saw what happened at the funeral. I was only there to mourn Lizzie. James is the one you should be talking to. He grabbed me at the funeral and began throwing me around. He's violent, you know? He threatened to kill me recently if he ever saw me again,' Rob explained.

'Tell us about your relationship with Lizzie, how long were you together?' Keeley asked.

'Let me think. Must have been just over five years. I first met Lizzie when I worked as a phlebotomist at Ipswich Hospital,' Rob continued.

Sergeant Morgan cut in, 'Can you please explain what a phlebotomist is, Mr Hoskins?'

'I take blood samples from patients, which are examined in a laboratory. That's how Lizzie and I met. She was donating blood at her school, and we struck up a conversation. She used to get anxious around needles, but I managed to keep her calm. About a month later, I ran into her at a bar where she was with her colleagues. We started talking, and from that point on, we just had an instant connection,' Rob explained

'Can you tell us about why your relationship ended?' asked Keeley.

Rob hesitated for a moment and then continued, 'Well, uh...sure. She moved in with me, and things were great. We made plans to buy our first house together and talked of getting married. But then things took a turn for the worse during the pandemic. I was furloughed from my job, and it hit me pretty hard. Eventually, I ended up losing my job as the demand for phlebotomists decreased, and their responsibilities were given to nurses. It was frustrating. I was in a bad place, started drinking, and took it out on her as she would carelessly spend what little money and savings we had together. I loved her and regret how I acted very much. I mean, hell, I never thought it would cause her to kill herself.'

Keeley nodded, jotting down notes. 'And what about Lizzie's sister? Did she have any role in your relationship?'

He clenched his jaw. Glancing around the room, his eyes avoided contact with anyone. Then he finally spoke, 'Lisa! Oh yeah, her! She had made it quite clear what she thought of me. There were times when Lisa tried to... influence Lizzie's decisions, let's say. As I mentioned, Lizzie struggled with managing her finances and Lisa would have to help her, she had made a bunch of money on the stock markets or something.'

'Mr Hoskins, that sounds like a significant source of tension. How did Lizzie respond to her sister's demands?' Sergeant Morgan probed.

Rob sighed heavily, his shoulders slumping. 'Lizzie was caught in the middle, you see? She loved her sister, of course, but she also resented the control Lisa seemed to exert over her life. She wasn't the easiest person to get along with, she would get all self-righteous with Lizzie about lending her money and would always offer the money with certain conditions attached. We had our disagreements about it. Lizzie was proud, she didn't want to be dependent on anyone, especially not her sister, but she had little choice when I lost my job I guess.'

'Thank you for being honest with us about this. We'll need to speak with Lisa as well to get a better understanding of the situation,' Keeley said.

Keeley shuffled in her seat. 'Mr Hoskins, did you ever get violent with Lizzie? Her sister is certain there were several complaints from neighbours.'

'Not sure what lies Lisa is spreading now about me!' Rob's eyes narrowed as he looked away for a moment before responding, 'Look, I'll be honest. Lizzie and I had our arguments like any couple. Yeah, there were times when things got heated, but it never led to violence.'

Sergeant Morgan turned back to Rob. 'Mr Hoskins, let's talk about that incident where you stole a van to evade the police. Can you explain your actions?'

Rob squirmed in his seat, avoiding eye contact, his fingers nervously tapping the tabletop. 'I... I panicked, okay? I saw you at the funeral, I thought you were there to confront me, and I didn't know what to do. So I ran. You had me cornered when I spotted the delivery van parked nearby, keys in the ignition. It was a stupid impulse. I jumped in and drove off as fast as I could. I didn't have a plan. I just wanted to get away from you. If I knew you were a police officer, I never would have run.'

Sergeant Morgan stated firmly, 'Mr Hoskins, stealing a vehicle is a serious offence. It raises questions about your actions and your state of mind—,'

'My client, still reeling from the recent loss of Miss Hargrave, found himself in an emotional state following the altercation at her funeral with her family,' Rob's lawyer interjected, leaning forward. 'Moreover, had PC Cooper unmistakably identified herself as an officer in uniform, the situation might have unfolded differently.'

Sergeant Morgan leaned forward, her eyes staring at the lawyer, 'Your client took off with a vehicle packed full of valuable items.'

Sergeant Morgan and the lawyer volleyed their arguments, each statement precise and sharp, like a tennis match at its peak.

'The vehicle has since been located and the company has confirmed nothing was taken. Therefore they have agreed to drop all of the charges on the basis that my client experienced genuine concerns regarding his personal safety,' the lawyer explained.

Keeley and Sergeant Morgan exchanged a knowing look, their eyebrows raising in silent acknowledgement.

As the interview came to an end, Keeley removed the tape from the recorder and sealed it in a box, ensuring its integrity. She asked everyone present to sign the sealed tape, confirming its authenticity. Rob concluded his discussion with his lawyer, and since the theft charge had been dropped, he was discharged due to insufficient grounds for further detention.

As she sat at her desk, lost in her thoughts, Keeley still couldn't shake the feeling that there was more to Lizzie's death than initially met the eye—despite the lack of concrete evidence. She found herself going over the details of the case repeatedly, searching for any overlooked clues or connections. Testimonies from Lizzie's family, the alleged violent history with Rob, and the unsettling admission that Lisa was somehow controlling Lizzie's life through money plagued her thoughts.

'What are you doing here today, Keeley? I thought you were meant to be off.'

Keeley looked up to see Sergeant Parker hovering over her.

She mustered a smile. 'I'm just working on a recent delivery van theft.'

Sergeant Parker let out a sigh, his expression softening. 'Is that so? Look, Keeley, I appreciate your dedication.' He paused for a moment, his hand absentmindedly scratching his bald head. 'Just remember, sometimes we have to prioritise our well-being. Speaking of well-being, I have a towering pile of reports to get to. Enjoy the rest of your time off when you get to it.'

Keeley knew she had to be careful. She couldn't let anyone, especially Sergeant Parker, know about her secret investigation. But the guilt of lying and the determination to uncover the truth weighed heavily on her conscience.

22

Keeley gathered her belongings and sat up from her desk ready to leave.

The persistent ring of the phone disrupted and froze her to the spot. 'What now?' she muttered under her breath.

'Hello,' she said, her voice tinged with irritation.

'Hello, PC Cooper,' the woman's voice replied.

Keeley clenched her fists. She paused, taking a deep breath, 'Mrs Bardwell? Is that you?'

'Yes. Yes, it is,' Mrs Bardwell replied, her voice sounding somewhat glum. 'I'm just calling to apologise if I sounded a bit standoffish the other day. Lizzie's death is affecting me more than I thought.'

'Don't mention it.' Keeley tightened her grip on the receiver. 'Your family's been through a lot lately,' she replied.

'I appreciate your understanding,' Mrs

Bardwell continued. 'But that's not my main reason for calling. I wanted to ask about what you mentioned—the possibility that Lizzie's death wasn't straightforward. I can't wrap my head around someone wanting to murder her. Have you found any evidence to suggest this?'

Keeley hesitated for a moment, thinking carefully. 'Mrs Bardwell, there was no evidence of a break-in or that someone could have drowned her without her resisting. I'm afraid Lizzie drowned herself, Mrs Bardwell.'

'But what about what the man said at the funeral?' Mrs Bardwell enquired, her voice breaking.

Keeley's curiosity was piqued. 'I'm confused. What man? Who have you been speaking to?'

'The funeral director we had in the beginning. He brought it up. He thought she could have been pulled into the bath and drowned. Now, what was his name? Hmm, I think his last name started with a W—maybe White?

'Whitford?' Keeley said, smiling to herself.

'Yes, oh, yes - that's the one! To my surprise, he turned up at the funeral before we went into the church. I must admit, his words have been nagging at me ever since. It's hard to fathom that she would take her own life. He seemed to think someone had murdered her. That must be nonsense, right?' responded Mrs Bardwell.

'It's an unlikely theory—'

'Rob? What about Rob?' asked Lisa.

'What about him?'

'He went to see Lizzie the night she died.'

'What? You never mentioned this the other day.'

'I've only just found out. Lizzie's neighbour called me. Something about seeing him shouting and banging on her door the night she died.'

'Do you have the neighbour's name and number to hand? I need to follow up on this,' Keeley asked, reaching across her desk for her pen and notepad.

Lisa hesitated. After a pause, she reluctantly offered the information, her voice wary.

Keeley jotted it down frantically.

'Rob, he must have...No, I mean, he couldn't have hurt her, could he?'

'Unlikely, we have just interviewed him. We will be sure to follow up on this information.'

'Wait, PC Cooper. Are you investigating this as a murder?'

'Mrs Bardwell, the case is closed. The coroner and Sergeant Parker have ruled it a suicide.'

'I see,' she said, her voice carrying an undertone of satisfaction. 'That is a relief to hear.'

Over the line, a stifled sob echoed, and it was followed by a prolonged silence.

Mrs Bardwell's voice cracked with emotion, 'I'm sorry, I can't continue this. Goodbye.' The call ended.

A sinking feeling gnawed at Keeley's stomach.

They had let Rob go. Frustration surged as she realised the lack of evidence to bring him in for questioning. Lisa's revelation about Rob showing up at Lizzie's door on the night of her death was a pivotal piece of information.

Keeley called the neighbour, but there was no answer. She left a voicemail, planning to try again the next day.

23

Keeley returned to the station after several days off, relishing the early morning solitude. At her desk, she focused on her new assignment—investigating a series of late-night shop thefts involving two men brandishing knives.

While Keeley was focused on the task at hand, a loud bang from the station entrance interrupted her peace. Her thoughts went to Sergeant Morgan, who frequently forgot her keys, causing such disruptions. Approaching the entrance, a sense of déjà vu clouded her mind.

Unlocking the door cautiously, Keeley was surprised to find Mr Whitford standing there.

'Mr Whitford. This better not be a joke! What brings you back?' Keeley asked.

His face settled into a resolute expression. 'There's been a murder.'

Keeley pushed back gently, recalling the previous incident. 'Miss Hargrave's death was ruled a suicide. There were no signs of foul play,' she countered, trying to assess the situation.

Undeterred, Mr Whitford's unwavering confidence remained. 'Not her. There's another body. Maybe I was wrong about Miss Hargrave, but I'm certain this one is not a suicide.'

Intrigued, Keeley pressed him for more information. 'What do you mean?'

Mr Whitford motioned for her to follow, leading her out to the car park. Memories of a previous encounter with him and his hearse flashed in her mind—the chilling image of a lifeless body, a shattered windscreen, and a veering car. She steeled herself and followed him to the rear of the vehicle not sure what to expect.

Keeley cautiously leaned over to get a glimpse inside the hearse.

'Damn it, Mr Whitford! Bringing this here again was a terrible mistake. I've already dealt with the fallout from Miss Hargrave's case.'

She hesitated, studying Mr Whitford's face before taking another look at the lifeless body. 'Right, here's the plan, Mr Whitford. You drive her to the pathologist's office and I'll follow. I'll call ahead to inform them of the urgency. I'll entertain your theory one last time. But if the pathologists determine it wasn't murder, you mustn't bring another body or make baseless claims again. Do you understand?'

'Sure, you're in charge. But, I'm not wrong,' Mr Whitford replied with a wry smile.

He got in his vehicle and set off ahead, leaving Keeley to return to the station to collect her belongings and lock up.

She took a deep breath, her grip tightened on the steering wheel, her knuckles turning white. 'Focus, Keeley,' she murmured to herself. 'Just breathe. I can do this!'

After calling the pathologist's office, she put the car in gear and set off.

24

Keeley hummed a tune under her breath, trying to calm her nerves as she drove to the coroner's office. This was the second corpse she had encountered recently. She focused on the task ahead, stressing the need for professionalism in the investigation.

As the coroner's office came into view, déjà vu struck Keeley for the second time. She parked next to Mr Whitford's hearse, and they exchanged glances before heading to the entrance and buzzing in.

Dr Pilkington emerged.

'Thank you, Dr Pilkington, for your assistance this morning. We appreciate it.'

They transferred the lifeless body onto the gurney and wheeled it towards an examination room, then onto the cold metal table.

Keeley studied the deceased woman, noting how her age and stature resembled her own, which raised questions about the woman's life and the circumstances of her tragic end.

'Let's see what we have here. Abrasions and ligature bruising around the neck,' Dr Pilkington said, examining the body.

As the examination continued, Dr Pilkington turned towards Mr Whitford, 'So, you're the funeral director causing all this trouble? Bodies should be put to rest, not taken to the police station,' he quipped.

Mr Whitford stared at Dr Pilkington, smirking. 'If you finish *your* job, I can finish mine,' he retorted.

Keeley smiled, appreciating the situation, and continued to inspect the body.

Dr Pilkington, ignoring Mr Whitford's remark, returned to the body, documenting his findings meticulously.

Turning to Mr Whitford again. 'So, Mr Whitford, do you have any details about the deceased and what happened?'

'Not much,' Mr Whitford replied. 'Her name is Sierra Watson, thirty-two years old. Her mother said she worked as a nurse. The porter at the hospital mortuary told me she was found hanging in her closet.'

Nodding in acknowledgement, Dr Pilkington clicked his recorder and resumed his examination. 'At the sternal end of the Sternocleidomastoid muscle, muscle fibre damage and haemorrhage can be seen.' He clicked the recorder and then turned to them both. 'It seems like a straightforward case of suicide by hanging. Many people use different items, looking at the marks they didn't use rope or a belt. If I had to guess it was likely a stole.'

Having absorbed this conclusion, Keeley redirected her attention to Mr Whitford. 'You disturbed me this morning and have dragged us all here, including Miss Watson. Can you explain to us all why you think she was murdered?'

Mr Whitford, undeterred, pointed to the body and continued, 'Gladly. If you care to look at her back under her armpits, you will see bruising similar to that of Miss Hargrave. Like she was dragged.'

Dr Pilkington moved with purpose, checking under each arm. Then, looking back at them both, he said, 'Yes, there's some very mild bruising, but I would say it's not as obvious as Miss Hargrave's. Again, nothing suspicious. We've moved this body already, and she would have been moved when she was found, so such marks may have formed post-mortem. Anything else more conclusive?'

'Yes, come look here. You can see some mild bruising here, where the skin has been punctured. Possibly an intravenous line has been placed in her arm.'

'Interesting. Perhaps she had surgery recently?' asked Keeley.

'Unlikely. It's not usually positioned here.

Often, they will inject a patient through a cannula, which is a thin plastic tube that feeds into a vein. This is usually on the back of your hand, as you can see no marks on her hands,' said Mr Whitford.

'You said she worked as a nurse, Mr Whitford? Could she have been misusing prescription drugs? I had a case a while back where a doctor was suffering from PTSD and overdosed on morphine.'

'Possible,' replied Mr Whitford.

'Let's think if she was regularly abusing drugs, she would try to conceal it. Let's check for pinpricks between her toes and fingers.' He carefully examined the feet, 'Here we go, come look here. Several pinpricks between the toes.'

Mr Whitford sighed, 'Damn, I missed that.'

'So, what are we saying?' asked Keeley.

Dr Pilkington replied 'She struggled with drug addiction and committed suicide. Not murder!'

Mr Whitford's shoulders sagged, and he released a defeated sigh. He turned away from the room, mumbling 'I'm sorry to have bothered you all with this. Please excuse me,' and left.

Keeley and Dr Pilkington discussed the next steps before returning the body to Mr Whitford's hearse. As he bid farewell and drove away, Keeley found herself questioning her previous judgement of him. What is he trying to achieve by insisting on these cases? The question continued to gnaw at her.

She decided to verify Dr Pilkington's assessment of Miss Watson's drug abuse as a nurse before moving forward and putting the two bodies and Mr Whitford's eccentric behaviour behind her. The tiny pinprick they found on Miss Watson's arm was nagging at the back of her mind. Was there more to it?

25

Keeley entered the hospital and approached the reception desk. The receptionist was busy looking through some files in a drawer.

Eventually, she noticed Keeley. 'Go down the corridor and take a left at the double doors, they're expecting you,' the receptionist said.

'Wait, what? You were expecting me?'

'Yes. Aren't you here about the incident in Ward 6A? I just got a report on it,' the receptionist said, her eyes scanning Keeley's uniform.

'Sorry, I'm confused. What happened in Ward 6A?' Keeley asked.

'Are you not here about the man who walked into the wrong room in gynaecology?' the receptionist recounted.

'Right. Sorry, I'm not here about that. I'm here on a separate matter. Could you point me towards the ward where Sierra Watson worked? I need to follow up on her recent suicide and speak to the ward matron.'

'I heard about that. Such a shame, she was so young. Let me just check which ward she worked on,' the receptionist said, as she moved towards her computer.

'Alright, here we go. She worked in our renal unit. You'll find it in the South Zone on the ground floor. Let me show you on the map,' the receptionist said, pointing out the location to Keeley.

Following the directions through the long, muted, maze-like hallways, Keeley made her way to the brown double doors with a sign reading "RENAL UNIT."

She pressed the buzzer and waited until she heard the door unlock. Entering the unit, she approached the reception desk and requested to speak with the ward matron.

After a few minutes, a serious-looking woman approached with curly brunette hair tied up in a ponytail and wearing mint green scrubs with a stethoscope slung around her neck.

'I'm Matron Edwards,' she said, pausing to rub her puffy eyes. 'You wanted to talk to me?'

Keeley extended her warrant card. 'PC Cooper, Lowestoft Police. I'm here to learn about Sierra. Could you share what you know about her?'

Matron Edwards nodded, her face stoic, hands folded across her chest, 'Sierra was hardworking, and patients liked her. A big loss to the team.'

'Did you notice any signs that she was struggling, either in her role or personal life?'

'Nothing specific.' Matron Edwards raised her hands, 'Look we deal with daily challenges and stress. There is support and counselling available if you need it,' Matron Edwards replied wearily.

Keeley nodded in understanding and continued, 'We found evidence suggesting Sierra may have been injecting herself with controlled drugs. Were you aware of this?' Keeley enquired.

'That can't be right,' Matron Edwards snapped. 'We have strict protocols and thoroughly vet our nurses. How dare you come here and accuse one of my nurses of such behaviour. Enough of this! I have a patient to prepare for a transplant. We're done here!' she declared, turning to leave.

After the abrupt ending, Keeley felt a wave of embarrassment. She offered an awkward smile and looked around the ward. She noticed a few patients and staff members glancing in her direction. Her eyes locked with those of a young nurse who had been staring at her.

Keeley's cheeks flushed as the nurse's curious stare bore into her. The young nurse offered a reassuring smile back to Keeley.

Approaching her with a friendly smile, Keeley scanned her name badge. 'Hi there... Kiara, I'm PC Cooper. I'm looking into Sierra Watson's case. Did you know her?'

Kiara hesitated for a moment, her eyes distant, before finally speaking. 'Well, we knew each other. Worked side by side for years. What happened to her, it's... it's just awful. I'm still struggling to process it all.'

'Can you think of anything that suggested Sierra was going through a hard time?'

Kiara hesitated, she looked at the floor, as she tried to find the right words. Each attempt to speak seemed to stall.

'You can tell me. I'm here to understand what led to her tragic end. I promise you won't get in any trouble,' Keeley reassured her.

Kiara explained, 'Well, there were moments when she seemed... distant, I guess. And quieter than usual. Then I caught her rifling through one of the locked medicine fridges looking for fentanyl. I confronted her, and at first, she tried to deny it, but she soon broke down in tears. She confessed that she had an addiction. I've known her since we trained together. Sierra was a good person, but she just had some bad luck recently. The loss of her mother, and seeing patients die each day was a constant reminder she told me. That can't have been easy! So I let it slide.'

Keeley nodded. 'Was Sierra in a relationship?'

Kiara paused, looking slightly uncomfortable. 'Well, in the past, she dated someone. I never liked him much. He was a lowlife. I met him a few times when we went out together.'

'Did he ever harm her? Physically, I mean?'

'I can't say for certain, but... There were occasions when she would come into work with bruises, and she would complain that he wasn't a nice man. I wouldn't put it past him. He was controlling and aggressive.'

'Can you remember his name?'

'Yes. Alex Thompson.' Kiara replied.

PC Cooper scribbled down the name and thanked Kiara for her time, she then started to head towards the ward exit.

'Excuse me, officer. There's something else. This morning, Sierra's grandad stopped by and asked me a bunch of questions like you. I forgot to tell you what I told him. Sierra mentioned to me she had started dating a colleague from the hospital.'

'Interesting. Do you know who it was?'

'Afraid not, she never told me who it was. Sorry, I can't be more helpful, I just thought you would need to know that.'

'Thank you for sharing that. It's odd that her family is investigating her past relationships. Can you describe Sierra's grandad to me?

'I thought it was strange too. I thought he was a patient because of the way he looked—white hair, thin, and wearing a suit and bow tie.'

Keeley smiled. 'I... I think I know him. Thank you again, Kiara, for your time. I must be off now.'

Returning from the hospital, she sat at her desk, replaying the conversation about Sierra's drug use in her mind.

The thought of Sierra's ex-boyfriend, Alex

Thompson, intrigued her.

Keeley decided to follow up on the colleague's remarks about Sierra's ex-boyfriend.

26

PC Seddon had agreed to accompany Keeley to Sierra's ex-boyfriend's address.

They exchanged glances outside the front door. Keeley knocked firmly, identifying them as police officers. The door creaked open, revealing a dishevelled man who appeared taken aback by their presence.

Keeley stared at him as she spoke, 'Mr Thompson? We need to talk to you about Sierra Watson.'

'Yeah. What's that cow been sayin' bout me? She's bare lyin', mate! All these things she said bout me, they're a bunch of lies!'

'Mr Thompson, may we come inside? This is concerning Ms Watson's recent suicide.'

Alex's face turned shocked and his initial hostility subsided. He opened the door wider for Keeley and PC Seddon to enter his cluttered living room.

Alex sat on the sofa, his head buried in his hands. 'What? Sierra... she... oh my god.'

'I understand this must be difficult for you, but we need to ask you some questions as part of our investigation.'

Alex shook his head, tears welling up in his eyes. 'I can't believe it. I had no idea...I never imagined...'

'Mr Thompson, we require your cooperation in answering a few questions. Let's begin with your relationship with Sierra and why it ended?' PC Seddon asked.

'Yeah, me and Sierra, we were a thing for a bit, innit? But, like, it didn't last, ya get me? She wanted all this fancy stuff and I ain't about that life, bruv. So, yeah, we had bare arguments and that,' Alex Thompson mumbled.

'During your time together, did you notice Sierra having a difficult time?' Keeley asked.

Alex thought for a moment and eventually replied, 'Nah, can't think of anything, mate. Her mum passing away was tough, though. Cancer at 55, innit? Proper shite luck, that.'

Keeley leaned forward, her eyes locked with Alex's. 'Mr Thompson, we have information that suggests incidents of violence between you and Sierra. Can you explain?'

'Nah, that ain't right!' Alex hesitated before continuing, 'Sierra's the one who got all physical with me. I dunno what you're on about.'

'I would prefer it if you were completely

honest with us, Mr Thompson. We do have witnesses who say otherwise, and the evidence does suggest that Sierra may have been a victim of domestic violence. Now, let's give that question another shot, or would you rather continue this conversation down at the station?' Keeley said.

Alex fidgeted uncomfortably, 'Nah, that's not needed. I never meant to hurt Sierra. We had our rows, yeah, but they never got that bad. I loved her, I swear.'

'Mr Thompson, our priority is to uncover the truth and bring justice to those involved. If there's more to the story, now is the time to share it.'

Alex hesitated, his eyes darting around the room like a caged animal. 'Sierra, you know, she was... going through some stuff. She had secrets, things she wouldn't tell me,' he admitted hesitantly. 'I tried to help her, but she just kept pushing me away.'

'Mr Thompson, we need to know the truth. Did you have any involvement in her death?'

Alex's facial expression conveyed distress as he responded, 'Nah, nah, man! I ain't seen her since we called it quits. I don't know what happened to her.'

'How long ago was that?' asked PC Seddon.

'Ugh, it's been nearly a year or something,' Alex muttered

'Did you know about a rumoured relationship

she was having at work?'

Alex visibly became uncomfortable. 'Like, I didn't really know much, ya know? Just bits and bobs from mates, innit? I heard she was seeing some bloke from the hospital, but that's all I got. I ain't seen her since we called it quits. If this bloke had anything to do with what happened to her you better lock him up. It's got nowt to do with me, swear down.'

PC Seddon and Keeley enquired about Alex's relationship with Sierra, possible motives and his whereabouts on the night of her death.

As Keeley and PC Seddon left Alex Thompson's house, Keeley turned to PC Seddon.

'I think we better double-check Thompson's alibi. Something about his story doesn't add up. What do you think?'

PC Seddon furrowed his brow. 'Agreed. I don't trust the lad. He couldn't get his story straight and openly lied to you about harming her,' he replied.

Keeley nodded acknowledging the inconsistencies in Thompson's story. Something about his manner suggested he was holding something back. She couldn't overlook the possibility of domestic violence or the fact that Thompson had been evasive about Sierra's personal struggles when questioned.

'Paul, there's one more thing. Can we try to obtain any CCTV footage from the night Sierra left work, the night of her death?'

'Will do.'

Back at the office, Keeley reviewed the evidence, including Sierra's case file and her relationship with Thompson. She was determined to learn more about Sierra's mystery relationship at work.

27

Cecil sat at his desk surrounded by images of the recent victims. The lamp's light cast an eerie glow on glossy A3-sized photographs. He meticulously scrutinised each one, examining every detail of their lifeless forms.

His obsession was evident as he examined every detail in each post-mortem image, studying the slim build and pale skin of the second victim, along with her freckles and light brown hair. He moved on to the photos displaying the abrasions and ligature marks around her neck. Was there something he wasn't seeing? Was there more to learn about her?

Once done, he carefully placed the photos back in their folder. Then turned his attention to another manila folder, removing several photos.

Cecil's brow furrowed as he observed the bruising and the colourless peeled skin of Lizzie's body shown in the photographs. With a frustrated sigh, he tossed them onto his desk, the glossy prints landing in a messy pile. He muttered to himself, 'Damn it, these are useless. I need to see that body again somehow.'

He considered his next steps carefully. Exhuming Lizzie Hargrave's body required a Home Office License, and he knew the family wouldn't agree to it. Convincing the coroner to conduct a thorough examination seemed unlikely after his discouraging talk with the forensic pathologist.

Suddenly, his attention snapped to the sound of footsteps outside his front door, shattering the eerie silence of the night. His mind raced. Was someone attempting to break in? He moved with stealth, back against the wall, staying in the shadows. A silhouette loomed at the front door, and the letterbox squeaked open, followed by a rustling sound as a small brown envelope slipped through.

The silhouette vanished, and he approached the door cautiously. Retrieving the letter, he examined it. The front was blank. Intrigued yet uneasy, he tore it open, revealing a single printed sheet that read, "*Cease your pursuit of Lizzie Hargrave. Her death was a suicide. You're delving into matters you shouldn't. Consider this your final warning!!!*"

Cecil unlocked the door and stepped out into the street, scanning up and down. Dead silence, no one in sight. He pondered who had sent this note, especially when only the family and the police were aware of his private crusade.

The implications were clear – someone wanted him to back off and stop prying into the details that didn't align with the official narrative. However, defying warnings was ingrained in his nature. This strengthened his resolve. The truth was out there, and he was determined to uncover it, despite the risks.

28

In the first light of morning, the sun cast its glow on the cemetery's wrought iron fences. Cecil tugged at his gloves as he walked through the gated entrance, his footsteps crunching on the gravel path.

A figure stepped into the sunlight, blocking the path ahead.

'Hey, stop right there, old man. What are you doing?'

'Stop messing around, Terry, we've got a job to do,' Cecil whispered.

'What's going on, Whitford? This seems dodgy.'

'It's perfectly fine. I forgot to remove a family heirloom before we buried her. Now the family wants it back. I'm going to need you to help get it back.'

Terry gave Cecil a sceptical look.

'Oh man, what are you like? You're getting on

in years. I've gotta ask, did you bring the needed licence?'

Cecil paused. 'Yes. Of course, it's right here.' He began searching his suit pockets. 'Nope, not in that pocket. Now where did I put it? This is embarrassing, I'm sorry, I must have left it back home. Can I give it to you next time I see you? You can trust me."

Terry let out a heavy sigh, before replying, 'Ummm. You know I'm supposed to have it. The new coroner's pretty strict about this stuff.' He ran his hand through his thick, wiry black hair. 'But, hey, since it's you, I'll cut you some slack. So, is this the one we're looking for, Hargrave?'

'Yes, that's the one.' Cecil replied as he inspected the polished granite headstone that read Lizzie Hargrave's name, date of birth, and date of death. A heartfelt message, *"Here lies a beloved daughter, sister, and teacher."*

Terry set to work, gently removing the tombstone and flowers. Finally, he dug down to the coffin, allowing Cecil access to the grave. As he descended into the freshly dug earth, he swiftly turned the sealing key.

In a few more weeks, he contemplated, her body would have begun its transformation. Cecil quickly began inspecting her feet and arms, searching meticulously for any unusual marks.

His heart raced at the sight of a faint bruise and a small skin puncture on the inside of her elbow. A victorious, though restrained, 'Bugger' escaped his lips, confirming his suspicions about the connection between the two cases.

'Did you say something, Whitford? Everything alright down there?

'Yes, Terry. Nearly done.'

'Good, hurry up, man. I'm freezing my bits off waiting.'

Speechless, Cecil struggled to make sense of what he had discovered. He was aware that he could not share his findings with anyone; he was alone in his pursuit of justice. He vowed to find justice for the two women.

Snapping back to the present, Cecil heard Terry's voice.

'Have you found it yet?'

'Yes, got it. Thank God. The family will be relieved,' Cecil said as he climbed out of the grave. 'Let's close her up and get her back underground.'

'Sure thing, bossman. Best be bringing me those papers,'

'Will do. Thanks again.'

'No more mistakes, Whitford. Maybe it's about time you retire before I'm digging you a hole?'

'Don't you worry, Terry, I've got plenty of time.'

Terry's laughter reverberated through the cemetery.

As Terry began the process of refilling the hole, Cecil followed the path back to his hearse, the weight of his discoveries pressing upon his thoughts.

He knew his next move, tracking down

the mysterious person mentioned by Sierra's colleague. Especially now he knew that the two suicides were linked.

29

PC Paul Seddon's eyes scanned the evidence files on his desk, his brow furrowed in concentration. He was focused on investigating Alex Thompson's alibi in relation to Sierra's death.

'Paul. Where's the Oscar report?' Sergeant Parker's stern voice interrupted his concentration, he placed his hands on his hips. 'Well? You said it would be ready for me to sign off yesterday!' Sergeant Parker barked.

'Urg...sorry sir. I got distracted by something else for Keeley. Give me a moment, I'll get to it now.'

'Make sure it's on my desk in the next hour.'

Paul watched as Sergeant Parker returned to his office, slamming the door shut behind him.

'God, what's got him in a huff,' he muttered under his breath.

He examined the report and evidence,

reflecting on the case. The evidence still pointed to suicide, with witnesses supporting Thompson's alibi. It appeared to be a straightforward case. Keen to move it along, he logged the unnecessary request for Ipswich Hospital CCTV footage from the night of Sierra's death, aware that it would likely take weeks to arrive.

He wondered about Keeley's motivations for pursuing a seemingly closed case. Was she seeking justice or striving to meet family expectations? He had seen it many times before, young officers often eager to prove themselves.

As he continued to sift through witness statements and evidence, PC Seddon felt a knot in his stomach. The evidence pointed to suicide, but he could sense that something was off. He wanted to help Keeley, but he also didn't want to lead her on. He was torn.

One aspect puzzled him: his investigation found no evidence of Sierra's involvement with anyone else. This fact struck him as odd, considering the interview with Alex Thompson. He decided it was likely nothing more than a rumour.

Reviewing the evidence, Paul reaffirmed his conclusions.

'Hey, Hannah, have you seen Keeley?' he shouted across the office, spotting Sergeant Morgan at her desk.

'Nope, she must be on patrol.'

'Got it,' PC Seddon replied as he flung his report on Keeley's desk.

He stood there, pondering if Keeley would accept his conclusion or persist in her pursuit.

Returning to his desk, he focused on Sergeant Parker's request.

30

He'd been a funeral director in Lowestoft for decades. The unexpected call from Sergeant Parker caught him off guard, instructing him to report to the police station. Unease gripped him as he parked and entered the station.

Stepping inside the station, he scanned the room. Fixing his eyes on the familiar sight of Charles Fitzgerald.

'For crying out loud!' he muttered.

'You!' The accusation rang out, and the plump little man approached, his beady eyes fixed on him with an unwavering intensity. His pointed finger aimed like a knight's lance, ready to pierce through the air and challenge him. 'What the hell do you think you're doing? This is outrageous!'

'Calm down, Charles. Let me explain.'

'You have no right to dig up a body without my permission! I'm the coroner of this county.

I'll...I'll... have you charged with desecration of a corpse!' Mr Fitzgerald's voice echoed through the corridor, drawing attention from others.

'Listen, I found some evidence the pathologists missed.'

'I don't care! You have no right to do this without my permission! I'm the one who decides if and when a body is exhumed!'

'I've not got time for this.' Cecil shook his head as he motioned to leave.

'Hold on.' Mr Fitzgerald grabbed Cecil's suit jacket. 'Don't think you can get away with this.'

Cecil grabbed his fingers in a lock and twisted his arm. 'Don't you ever dare touch me again, Charles,' he spoke in a soft voice, his cold stare fixed on the trembling Coroner of Suffolk.

'Will you two pack it,' commanded Sergeant Parker. 'You're making a scene in my station.'

'You should arrest him, David. Do you know what he has done?' Mr Fitzgerald said in a high-pitched voice.

'Yes, yes. Half the blooming station heard you both. I agree, what Mr Whitford did was unorthodox, but I'm confident he won't do it again.'

'No way. He's not getting away with this. His theatrics need to be punished!'

Sergeant Parker looked pleadingly towards Mr Whitford, 'Anything you have to say about the situation, Mr Whitford.'

Cecil shrugged.

'I know. Perhaps a fine would suffice?' Sergeant Parker suggested.

Mr Fitzgerald clenched his fists and leaned closer to Mr Whitford, his voice dropping to a dangerous whisper. 'Very well. But let me make this crystal clear, Mr Whitford. If you do anything like this again, you'll find yourself in a world of trouble you can't even imagine. I'll be watching your every move, and any misstep will have consequences you won't be able to escape. Don't forget that.' With a final glare, he turned and left.

Mr Whitford let out a deep sigh and his lips curled into a triumphant smile.

'I'm curious, Sergeant Parker. Why did you help me back there?'

Sergeant Parker paused, considering the question. 'Well if you must know. When I saw you recently the morning you brought Miss Hargrave's body, I couldn't place where I remembered you from. It wasn't until I got home that evening and saw my wife, it dawned on me. You were the funeral director when we buried my mother-in-law. Consider this a favour repaid.'

Cecil thanked him and turned to leave the station.

'Hold it right there, Mr Whitford,' Sergeant Parker called out. 'I appreciate your intention to help, but it's important to acknowledge that you've become somewhat of a nuisance around town recently. Both of these cases are suicides, nothing more. Leave the police work to the professionals. You're delving into matters you shouldn't. Consider this your final warning.'

Cecil nodded solemnly. 'Understood,' he replied.

Walking to his car, Cecil couldn't help but think about his future as a funeral director in Lowestoft. His actions could have potentially harmed his reputation and business, he had been fortunate to have gotten away with just a fine.

Though he couldn't turn a blind eye if there was even a slight possibility of two unsolved murders. With conflicting emotions of relief and caution, Cecil left the police station, vowing to exercise more prudence in his pursuit of the truth.

31

Unconscious, the body lay motionless from the effects of the sevoflurane. He stood over the figure, observing its vulnerable form. The dimly lit room cast eerie shadows, intensifying the gravity of his actions.

He thought, perhaps the circumstances of Lizzie's death were necessary; Sierra's fate could, perhaps, have been avoided, he thought to himself, as he dragged Sierra into the bathroom, reminiscent of the night he had ended Lizzie's life.

He felt a surge of frustration looking down at Sierra's lifeless body and then at her bathtub. Delivering a forceful kick to the small bathtub, the sound echoed through the room.

'No! No, no. Damn it!' he roared.

Realising the small bathtub wouldn't suffice, he panicked, his mind racing for alternatives.

He quickly moved Sierra's lifeless form to the bedroom. The room felt suffocating, and the sound of his own laboured breathing echoed in his ears. In a frenzy, he cleared the wardrobe, clothes falling haphazardly to the floor. He reached for a stole hanging there.

He positioned Sierra's limp body against the wardrobe, looping the stole around her neck and securing it tightly.

Stepping back to admire his work, his eyes widened as he stared at her for a long moment. His lips curled into a faint smile. He glanced at his watch, after which he turned and left the room, but not before pausing at the doorway to cast one final glance at her slumped defeated form.

'Excuse me, hello.'

The petrol service assistant's shrill voice brought him back to the present. She repeated herself.

'£40.99 for pump 2,' she said.

'Sorry, I'm a million miles away,' he replied, tapping his card on the reader.

He glanced at the plump woman. She was wearing a fluorescent yellow and red fleece. He scanned her with detachment.

'That has all gone through. Have a nice day.'

'I'll try,' he snarked back before heading to his car, a faint smile on his lips.

32

'I'm on their tail. The suspect is driving a bright green Seat Ibiza. Last seen near the petrol station on Bridge Road. He just turned onto London Road,' PC Carter relayed.

Keeley and Sergeant Morgan sped down High Street, their patrol car's siren cutting through the air. The radio scanner crackled with PC Carter's updates.

'We're approaching your position,' replied Sergeant Morgan.

She tightened her grip on the steering wheel. This was her first vehicle pursuit and she was determined to prove herself.

PC Carter's voice crackled again as he asked 'Do you have a visual? I've lost sight of the suspect.'

'Negative. We're closing in on your position,' replied Sergeant Morgan.

'Hold on tight!' Keeley exclaimed, a surge of excitement and nerves coursing through her.

The wailing siren echoed through the streets as they weaved through the traffic, causing cars to brake sharply to make way for them.

Keeley's eyes widened as she spotted the bright green Seat Ibiza in the distance. It was only a few cars ahead now, and she could see the driver weaving in and out of traffic recklessly.

'We've got him. What is the suspect wanted for?' asked Keeley.

'Reported burglary on Elm Tree Road,' said PC Carter.

'He's heading north-west down Milton Road.'

Keeley slammed her foot down on the accelerator, the engine roared as the Vauxhall Vectra lurched forward. The tyres squealed in protest as she swerved in and out of traffic, closing the gap between them and the Seat Ibiza. Her hands shook as she navigated the patrol car through the chaotic traffic on London Road South. She could feel the jolt of the speed bumps beneath the tyres and the screech of the brakes as she came to a sharp turn.

'Right! Right! Right!' commanded Sergeant Morgan.

Keeley jerked the steering wheel to the right, and the Vauxhall Vectra attempted to follow the Seat Ibiza as it exited the roundabout at speed. But luck was not on their side.

'You little bugger! Hang on...' Keeley swore, her determination undeterred. They couldn't let the suspect escape.

Keeley swerved the car sharply, narrowly avoiding multiple vehicles. The sudden turn jolted her and Sergeant Morgan forward in their seats, their seatbelts digging into their chests. The engine died out and the siren immediately silenced as the car screeched to a halt. Keeley slammed her hand against the steering wheel, making a loud beep. She then swiftly restarted the engine, slammed it into gear, and resumed the pursuit.

Ahead, the Seat Ibiza began to slow down as it encountered rush-hour traffic, all of a sudden braking and taking a left turn onto Waveney Drive.

With a burst of speed, she closed the distance, skillfully manoeuvring to pull up alongside it.

'Oh no, oh no,' Keeley blurted out as they raced towards the dead end at breakneck speed.

The road ahead was closed for road work, blocked by a set of metal gates adorned with various stop signs.

'Brake, brake, Keeley stop the car!' Sergeant Morgan cried out.

Bracing herself, Keeley slammed on the brakes, the car screeching to a halt just in time.

The Seat Ibiza swerved towards the dead end at speed. She watched in horror as it crashed into the metal barriers, sending sparks flying.

'Fuck me! That was close,' Sergeant Morgan said, turning to Keeley, her voice still trembling with adrenaline.

Keeley slumped back in her seat, her breath coming in ragged gasps.

PC Carter's vehicle joined them moments later, pulling up alongside Keeley's car. Winding down his window, he remarked 'What a mess! I'll start getting these crowds back. Morgan, can you call for an ambulance?'

Sergeant Morgan nodded and made the call.

As the commotion settled, the distant wail of an approaching ambulance grew louder by the second, its flashing lights soon illuminated the scene, casting an eerie glow over the damaged vehicles and the concerned faces of onlookers. Keeley and PC Carter quickly worked to disperse the gathering crowd.

Sergeant Morgan, followed by Keeley, made her way to the scratched driver's side of the Seat Ibiza, assessing the situation.

'Wait a minute...I know that driver!' Sergeant Morgan said.

Keeley approached the driver's side, peering inside. 'Oh my God!' Keeley exclaimed in surprise as she saw Rob Hoskins slumped over the deflated airbag, unconscious.

33

After blue-lighting through the busy streets of Lowestoft, they screeched into a bay outside A&E. Keeley and Sergeant Morgan followed the paramedics to a hospital bed, where they transferred Rob.

Shortly after, a nurse in a yellow gown and blue gloves closed the privacy curtain, providing a moment of calm amidst the chaos.

'Who do we have here, officers?' the nurse enquired.

'Mr Robert Hoskins, 37.'

The nurse turned her attention to Rob's handcuffed hands on the bed, then shifted her focus to her tablet, her fingers tapping frantically.

'What happened to him?'

'He was involved in a car accident when attempting to evade us. He crashed into roadworks.'

'Remind me never to get on your bad side, officers,' the nurse smiled.

Her fingers rapidly tapped on the tablet, reviewing the information and then checking the monitor.

'His vitals appear stable. No critical injuries are indicated. We'll need to perform a CT scan, so we'll have to remove the handcuffs. You can stay and monitor, but rest assured, he won't be going anywhere in his current state,' she said.

Keeley glanced briefly at Rob on the bed, the adrenaline-fuelled car chase replaying in her mind.

'I'm going to stretch my legs and get a drink. Would you like something too?'

'Good idea. Tea with two sugars, please,' Sergeant Morgan replied, her attention unwavering on Rob.

Grateful for the brief break, Keeley nodded and exited the trauma ward, heading towards the hospital cafeteria.

However, as she walked through the bustling hallway, her steps slowed, and her posture sagged. The adrenaline that had fuelled her during the car chase was fading, replaced by creeping exhaustion.

Keeley's stomach churned as she raced for the toilet. She stumbled into a cubicle and collapsed over the bowl, her body heaving as she emptied the contents of her stomach. Her body shook from the physical exertion, but it was the emotional aftermath of her first car chase that made her hands tremble.

After a few minutes of collecting herself and wiping away the only remaining streak of vomit from her face, she exited the cubicle. She rinsed her mouth out with water from the sink and splashed cool water onto her face.

Looking at herself in the mirror, she straightened her uniform, taking several deep breaths before saying to herself 'You're okay.'

After leaving the toilets, she approached the cafeteria counter, drawn by the aroma of freshly brewed coffee and the hum of conversation.

As she made her way back to the trauma ward. The hospital corridors buzzed with activity as medical personnel rushed past, a perpetual reminder of life's fragility.

34

Cecil parked Angel in a vacant space, his mind focused on the gamble he was about to take. He had visited this place several times recently, wondering if they would listen to him.

Pressing the buzzer, he said 'I'm here to see Dr Pilkington, please.'

With a heavy sigh, a voice replied, 'Is he expecting you, sir?'

'No. If you can tell him that Mr Whitford is here to see him, thank you.'

'One moment, sir.'

He could hear the receptionist continuing her conversation with someone else.

'Yes, we've got an unannounced visitor downstairs. He says his name is Mr Whitford. Yes, yes, okay, in that case, I'll send him up now.' She pressed the button to unlock the door. "Dr Pilkington will see you now.'

Cecil smiled to himself as he walked into the

reception area. The receptionist gave him a tired look.

'Thank you. You have a lovely day now,' Cecil said. He proceeded down the familiar corridor.

Reaching the door of the room where they had examined Sierra Watson's body, Cecil knocked firmly.

'Come in, Mr Whitford,' came Dr Pilkington's voice from within.

Cecil instinctively scanned his surroundings, stepping into the room.

Dr Pilkington leaned back in his chair, his fingers drumming on the desk. His eyes locked onto Cecil for a moment, before he spoke. 'Any more bodies for me today or is it a slow day at the office?' Dr Pilkington chuckled.

Cecil remained composed. 'Not today, but I do have something interesting to share that I wanted to get your advice on.'

'I'm listening,' Dr Pilkington replied, leaning in closer.

'I found the same puncture mark on Miss Hargrave's body, just like the one on Miss Watson's. It was faint but clear, and we missed it.'

Dr Pilkington's brow furrowed, his face a mixture of surprise and confusion. 'Wait, what? Slow down. How did you see this? Last time I checked, she was six feet deep in the ground.'

'She is. But this morning I had a quick look at her.'

Dr Pilkington's expression twisted with

concern. 'You did what? How on earth did you pull that off? The coroner's office will have a meltdown if they catch wind of this!'

Cecil sighed, 'That doesn't matter. What truly matters now is that it reveals a connection between the two apparent suicides, and I'm increasingly convinced they weren't suicides at all.'

Dr Pilkington studied Cecil, processing the new information. He was intrigued by what the old fool had to say.

'Okay, let's say hypothetically they weren't suicides and someone caused both deaths. What do you need my help with?'

'I wanted to get your thoughts on the marks. I'm thinking they look like needle marks.'

'Agreed, Mr Whitford, they do appear to be marks made by a syringe. Although we know the nurse appeared to be using drugs. Maybe the first victim was also using drugs?'

'Our theory was partially correct. The nurse was using prescription drugs. I visited the hospital and spoke to a colleague. This explains the hidden marks you found between her toes. But the other mark is not hidden. So, humour me, let's say the murderer used a syringe on her. What do you think they gave her? I'm thinking, some form of sedative.'

'That would explain how a murderer could move them to where they wanted. The bathtub is being used to stage drowning, and the wardrobe is for hanging.'

'Could it also explain the closed mouth with a small amount of froth?' Cecil posed.

Dr Pilkington nodded.

'So, what would you give someone to make them unconscious enough to drown them?' asked Cecil.

'Something strong. I would guess a general or local anaesthetic like prilocaine would do the trick. This would not be something we screen for on the toxicology we got back on each victim.'

'So, would this imply the perpetrator either worked in a hospital or had an accomplice with access to it?'

'Agreed, Mr Whitford. Are you considering involving the police? That young officer seemed interested in assisting.'

'I can't do that at this point. There's a lack of evidence to support this theory, and I've lost credibility with the police and the coroner's office,' Cecil explained. 'But I recently spoke to a young nurse who mentioned that there's a phlebotomist at the hospital who knew the nurse. They work closely together, so there's a chance they might be our murderer or have an idea of who else might want them dead.'

Dr Pilkington considered the new information. 'Phlebotomist? That's an unexpected lead, but it makes sense. They have access to medical supplies and could potentially administer sedatives. What's your next move?'

Cecil nodded earnestly. 'I need to find that phlebotomist. They might hold the key to unravelling this mystery. Thank you for your insights, Dr Pilkington.'

With their discussion concluded, Cecil headed back to Angel. He started the engine and made his way to the hospital, determined to pursue this lead.

35

He parked in Car Park 1 and then headed to the reception desk.

'Hello, I was hoping you could help. I'm looking for Rob Hoskins. I believe he works here?'

'I'm sorry, sir, but we cannot disclose the whereabouts or details of our staff members to visitors. Not without proper authorisation or a legitimate reason in accordance with hospital policy.'

'Oh, no. Sorry, I should have made myself clearer. You see, he's my grandson. He's expecting me today. He asked me to stop by. He has offered to help me with a medical issue. It's rather painful, you see.'

'Unless you have an appointment I cannot help you.'

Cecil leaned over the reception desk and whispered, 'I have a large abscess on my anus that needs to be drained. Very discomforting, my dear. Is that enough proof, or do you need to see it?'

'Oh my gosh! Right, let me see where Mr Hoskins is in the hospital right now,' the receptionist uttered as she began frantically tapping away at her computer.

'He's on Floor One. Trauma & Orthopaedics. You poor thing, hope you get it sorted.'

Cecil nodded with a sincere smile. Then headed to the double lifts. Pressing the button for the lift, he waited, shifting uncomfortably on the spot, as his eyes darted around the busy setting, the familiar smell of antiseptic that permeated every inch of the place. 'I hate hospitals,' he muttered under his breath.

The doors finally opened and he entered the lift, pressing the button for floor one.

Lost in a trance as the smooth jazz lift music lulled him, he was jolted back to the present. The hallways were crowded, nurses paced with purpose as their feet squeaked on the floor, and muffled discussions occurred amongst visitors and medical staff.

'Mr Whitford?'

He turned in the direction of the voice calling him. He scanned her tired face, noticing the dark circles under her eyes.

'What are you doing here?' she asked.

'Oh...PC Cooper. Hello again. I didn't expect to see you here. What am I doing here? Oh, yes, of course. I'm visiting a friend.' He leaned in closer, his words barely audible. 'Nasty abscess, nothing serious'.

'I'm sorry to hear that...'

'Cooper! Cooper! Quick, get over here now!' A frantic female voice echoed across the ward.

Keeley began sprinting across the ward, ripping back the curtain, to be met with pandemonium. She watched as nurses frantically circled Rob, yelling commands to one another as the monitor beeped furiously.

'37-year-old male, experiencing sudden breathing difficulties. Mr Hoskins...Mr Hoskins!' said a nurse as she shook him by the shoulders and spoke loudly to him in an attempt to rouse him.

Another nurse called out, 'Starting chest compressions.' The room filled with the rhythmic sound of her hands pressing down on the sternum, accompanied by the audible count, 'One, two, three, four...'

'Molly, I need you to secure an IV and administer 1 mg of epinephrine!' one nurse instructed another.

Mr Whitford curiously made his way over. Scanning the scene unfolding in front of him, he began to read the monitor. Cecil looked closer and saw that the vital signs had fallen outside of the normal range. An alarm sounded and an alert was flashing on the screen.

Looking at the chart, he could see it was likely asystole; he knew from his training that this was not shockable using a defibrillator and that if he did not respond to BLS and ACLS treatments, he would be dead.

After several more compressions and the nurses administering further epinephrine every three minutes, they all stopped. 'It's hopeless, he's gone. I'm calling it,' one of the nurses replied.

Keeley stood there in disbelief as Rob Hoskins lay motionless in his hospital bed.

'Damn it! He was stable just moments ago! What the hell happened?' Sergeant Morgan exclaimed, turning to look at Keeley.

Cecil shuffled alongside Keeley, 'Who's this, may I ask?'

'I shouldn't be telling you this, but seeing as it makes no difference now, this is Lizzie Hargrave's ex-boyfriend. He used to work at the hospital here as a phlebotomist.'

'No way. What was his name? Did you say he worked here?'

'Rob Hoskins. No, he doesn't work here anymore, was let go a while ago. We had just found out he knew Sierra also, he seemed to be the only common link between two unrelated suicides. Pointless now.'

Cecil thought about what this meant. Rob was the only connection between the two cases. Could he have killed both women? He had access to drugs that could have been used to incapacitate the victims.

36

'Thank you for your time, officers. If you'll excuse me, I must be going to see my friend before visiting hours close. Good to see you again PC Cooper, you take care now.'

'Of course, Mr Whitford. I hope your friend is okay,' said Keeley.

He exited the trauma ward and headed up the stairs, following the signs to the anaesthesia department. Cecil peered through the glass panel of a door and saw a man sitting at his desk, feet propped up, engrossed in his phone.

Cecil knocked firmly on the door. The man in the chair swivelled around to face him.

The anaesthesiologist—a man in his early forties with short-cropped hair and navy wire-rimmed glasses—stared back at him.

'Are you lost, sir?' the anaesthesiologist asked assertively.

Cecil replied with a wry smile, 'I don't think so.

I believe this is the anaesthesia department, isn't it?'

Intrigued, the anaesthesiologist removed his feet from the desk, becoming more attentive. 'Yes, it is. What do you need?'

Cecil began, 'I'd like to pick your brain about something. I used to work as a medic in the Royal Navy. There was a case from my past that I've been thinking about recently. A soldier drowned, and I oddly found a needle mark on his hand. The toxicology report showed no traces of any known drugs. As an anaesthesiologist, I thought you might have some insight?'

'Interesting. Any signs of foul play?'

'No,' Cecil replied, shaking his head. 'He left a suicide note. What intrigued me most was the needle mark on his hand. How could someone render themselves or another person unconscious enough to drown?'

'Well, let's discuss it hypothetically. If I were to render someone completely unconscious, I would use a general anaesthetic. It would achieve the desired effect and it would not show on a regular toxicology, not unless they were looking for it,' the anaesthesiologist explained.

Cecil listened intently, nodding as he absorbed the information given. 'How would he have obtained access to that?' he asked.

'It can only be administered in a hospital setting. Of course, it's very difficult for someone to get a hold of. We keep it secure in our drug cupboards. These are locked whenever the operating theatre is unoccupied.'

Cecil expressed his gratitude to the doctor and took his leave. Standing in the hallway, he contemplated the revelation. Could it be as simple as the man he had just witnessed die being the mastermind behind the recent suicides? He had access to drugs and knew both victims. Perhaps karma had caught up with him, and justice for Lizzie and Sierra was now out of reach.

The revelation about Rob Hoskins sent his mind spinning, but a nagging thought tugged at the corners of his consciousness. Something didn't add up. While it was clear that Rob had the means and likely had the opportunity to harm both Lizzie and Sierra, the motive remained a mystery.

What he couldn't understand was if Rob no longer worked at the hospital, how did he access the drugs? Unless he had help from someone else?

As Cecil drove away from the hospital, he knew he couldn't let it go, not with so many questions still left unanswered.

37

'What a day, Keeley!' exclaimed Sergeant Morgan. 'I need another one of these,' she said, tapping her empty cocktail glass with her finger. All that was left was melted ice and a grapefruit wedge.

'I know, right? I've never experienced so much action and death,' responded Keeley.

'Today was insane! Never been in a car chase like that before,' said Sergeant Morgan. 'You handled yourself like a pro out there.'

Keeley smiled back.

She thought to herself how these experiences were what she had always craved, but the toll they were taking on her was unexpected. Seeing Mr Whitford again and reflecting on his military record made her wonder. The man must have seen his fair share of deaths and now handled the dead. She couldn't help but question herself – could she handle being surrounded by so much death on a daily basis?'

'Right, what can I get you? Same again?'

Keeley hesitated, her eyes scanning the menu. 'Seeing as I'm not on duty tomorrow,' she mused, her brow furrowing slightly. 'Yes, I'll have another vodka, lime, and soda, please.' Her fingers lightly tapped the menu as she spoke. She had always been more comfortable with her own company or with a select few trusted individuals, making the process of ordering somewhat unfamiliar to her.

Hannah gracefully slid out of the booth and executed a slight, playful bow, her smile brimming with mischief. Keeley's gaze remained on her as she headed to the bar.

Keeley scanned the room, which was almost empty except for a few lonesome men perched in the booths with tall pints.

The Paradise Escape Lounge was unusually quiet for a weeknight. Keeley had visited this place before with Hannah on weekends, both during and outside of work hours. Often breaking up several fights or dealing with hen parties that had gotten out of hand whilst on duty.

One of the flat-screen televisions played a newly released music video. The female singer paraded around a luxury villa, singing about being wronged and buying herself flowers. Keeley smiled to herself; she had been single since she had completed her apprenticeship over a year ago. Having had a few flings, she was not looking to settle down, she kept reminding herself that she was only 21 and had plenty of time to find someone. The job didn't leave much time or inclination for other things, she thought, especially buying herself flowers.

She peered back towards the bar, wondering why it was taking so long despite the emptiness of the place. Noticing Hannah being coerced by some man she had just met reminded her this was a typical night out with Hannah, which often meant she would end up sitting alone, scrolling through her social media stories, while batting away a sea of men who tried to chat to her.

As the evening wore on, the room gradually filled with patrons occupying booths and tables. Keeley's attention, however, was drawn to a couple seated at the back of the room, and she immediately recognised one of them. She observed them closely, her mind buzzing with questions about their relationship and why they had chosen to meet at a bar. Maybe it was all innocent, she thought, her tendency to overanalyze situations getting the best of her. Perhaps they were just friends or colleagues.

But then, her suspicions were confirmed as she watched the young woman's hand slide up the man's leg beneath the table. Disappointment and distaste welled up inside Keeley. The woman's laughter and their exchanged devilish grins only intensified her feelings.

Keeley was hit by a sudden memory, sharp and clear—the time she had discovered her then-girlfriend with her university roommate—a reminder that sometimes it was better to let things go.

Despite her increasing curiosity about their interaction, Keeley knew the importance of maintaining professionalism as a police officer in public. Yet, an inexplicable urge surged within her, compelling Keeley to approach their table. She imagined a scenario in her head, where she confronted them.

'Hello... Hello... Earth to Keeley. You all right, mate? Something interesting going on over there?' Sergeant Morgan interrupted, snapping her back to reality.

'Sorry, daydreaming. See that man over there?' Keeley said, gesturing towards the couple.

'Quite the looker, wouldn't mind a bit of that. Unfortunately, he looks taken with Barbie there,' remarked Sergeant Morgan.

'No, you've gotten it wrong. He's not my type! I'm watching him because he's connected to a case I've been working on recently. He's married, and that's not his wife he's with tonight.'

'What a jerk! Men! Only good for three things in life!'

'Oh... yeah? What are they?' asked Keeley.

'Well, of course, spider-killing, shelf-reaching, and sex,' Hannah replied with a smirk.

Keeley burst into laughter. 'Yeah, I agree. We don't need men. Right, what happened to my drink order? Did you get distracted by the gentleman at the bar?'

Hannah grinned sheepishly. 'Oh, him? He seemed nice. He offered to take me out next week. But, getting back to us, I totally forgot about our drinks. How about we ditch this place and grab a burger?'

Keeley's laughter tapered off as Sergeant Morgan brought up the man at the bar. A faint crease appeared on her forehead. She shifted her gaze to Hannah and finished the remains of her drink, her eyes not meeting Hannah's with the same warmth as before.

'Yeah. Sure, let's do that. I'm so hungry I could eat a scabby monkey,' she replied.

Heading toward the exit, Keeley couldn't help but notice James Bardwell deeply engaged in conversation, seemingly oblivious to her presence. Thoughts about his situation and its potential impact on her own life swirled in her mind. However, she resisted the urge to confront him, even though she had briefly entertained the idea. She wondered whether Lisa knew about her husband's infidelity. With a wistful glance, she trailed behind Sergeant Morgan, making her way out of The Paradise Escape Lounge.

38

Cecil found no solace in sleep; instead, he tossed and turned beneath his rumpled bed sheets. Unresolved questions kept him awake. He reached for his pocket watch on the nightstand. Its polished brass surface glinted in the dim moonlight filtering through the curtains, revealing the time – 2 a.m. The night dragged on, and his mind continued to buzz with the anticlimactic conclusion following Rob Hoskins' death.

Sitting up in bed, restlessness gnawed at him. He had combed through the evidence and theories, finding no other leads. Perhaps his investigation had genuinely reached its end. He attempted to calm his racing thoughts, resting his head back down on the pillow.

Shortly after, he sat bolt upright, heart pounding, and swiftly leaped out of bed. He moved swiftly through the darkness to reach his study.

'Now, where did I put that?' he said to himself as he frantically pulled each drawer open and sifted through the stacks of documents that adorned his desk.

'There it is,' he declared as he pulled a brown envelope from his desk drawer. He held it under his desk lamp, examining the note inside several times.

"Cease your pursuit of Lizzie Hargrave. Her death was a suicide. You're delving into matters you shouldn't. Consider this your final warning!!!"

The author of the printed letter remained an enigma. Cecil pondered if the man he had seen in the hospital bed had written it to deter him from the truth.

Frustrated and burdened with more unanswered questions than before, he placed the letter back into its envelope and flung it into the desk drawer.

Then, in the soft glow of his desk lamp, he noticed something peculiar.

Grabbing the envelope again, he held it closer to the lamp, revealing a lone hair—an enigmatic thread connecting him to the elusive sender. There was a trail to follow, and his instincts urged him not to cease his pursuit of the truth just yet.

39

The Brentwood train journey felt excessively long due to reduced services due to train strikes, causing a delay. Keeley stood among the restless crowd and shifted her weight from one foot to the other, scanning for a vacant seat at each stop.

Finally, a seat opened up, but an elderly woman, whose snoring resembled that of a congested pig, took it.

Just as Keeley thought the ordeal couldn't get any worse, the elderly woman abruptly woke up, rustling a pack of tuna sandwiches and beginning to munch away. The strong fishy smell filled the air. Keeley grimaced and let out a sigh of relief as the train finally pulled into Chelmsford. Eagerly, she made her way to switch for the final leg of her journey.

Shenfield train station greeted her with weathered red bricks, and a sign proudly announcing, "Welcome to Shenfield" above its entrance.

As the train came to a halt, she disembarked and ascended the stairs, crossing the walkway to reach the opposite platform.

The rain, which had been looming ominously, now fell heavily upon her. The sky turned into a grey blanket, and rain poured down, drenching her clothes in seconds. She cursed herself for forgetting to bring a coat and sprinted across the car park towards her dad's Jaguar X-Type, a racing green pearl, as he often emphasised. Her hair stuck to her forehead as rain ran down the contours of her nose.

Reaching the car, she pounded on the window. Inside, her dad fumbled with the buttons, his silhouette barely visible in the darkness as he struggled to unlock the car. Finally, the lock clicked open. She swung the door wide and climbed into the passenger seat, the brown leather squelching beneath her wet clothes.

'Hi, Dad. Thanks for picking me up.'

'Anytime, Keels. You're soaked, dear. Where's your coat? Have you eaten yet?' her dad asked.

'I'm fine, stop worrying. I ate earlier, just tired.' A weary smile formed on her lips.

'Sorry, sorry. I forgot you are a grown woman.'

Her dad started the engine, flicking on BBC 2. *The Folk Show* with Mark Radcliffe softly played in the background, its soothing melodies providing a calming backdrop to their conversation.

Keeley reached for the heater controls, her chilly fingers struggling to adjust the temperature gauge. As warm air gradually filled the car, she began to rub her hands together to generate some warmth.

'So, how's things, Dad? What have you been up to?'

'Not much, just the usual. Work and boring jobs around the house. We had a leak in the loft recently, which was a nightmare.'

'Oh no, that's awful. I presume the airport is busier again?'

'Yeah, it seems that way. Long queues are back, but they recently laid off some people. I'm trying to lie low as I can't afford to lose my job. Who else would want to hire a 49-year-old ex-military?' He sighed, the weight of his words palpable.

'You're selling yourself short. You have a lot of valuable skills, Dad, and many companies actively seek to hire ex-military personnel.'

'Yeah... I suppose that's true. Although, most people who do that usually have IT or engineering backgrounds. I find my work in security quite enjoyable.'

'What else have you been up to?'

'Well, I've actually been getting back into bird-watching lately. Do you recall when you were a kid, and we used to visit Cattawade?'

'Erm, not that one. I vaguely recall a site with a funny name. What was it called... oh yes! "The Sponge," do you remember that one?'

'Oh yeah! You loved that place. Good times. I remember that was the one with the seasonal pools, perfect for passage waders.'

'How's mum doing? I've not heard from her recently,' Keeley asked, seeking a change of subject.

Her dad briefly glanced away from the road, weariness and concern evident in his eyes. 'You know, long hours and tough work,' he replied.

'I know, Dad. I'm a police officer too.'

'Of course, of course, Keels,' her dad said, his eyes refocusing on the road.

'If you must know, it's been a tough couple of weeks at work for me. I've been dealing with a series of suspicious deaths. It's frustrating because everyone is trying to dismiss them as suicides,' she shared with a sigh.

'That's a tough job you have there, Keels. I remember when you first told me you wanted to join the police force. I was worried sick. I've seen what it has done to your mum,' her dad admitted, adding, 'But remember, it's not a competition.'

'I know, but it's something I'm passionate about. I want to make a difference, and I feel like I'm doing that.'

'You've always been determined, Keels. I'm proud of you. Don't let others make you second-guess yourself. If you're onto something, don't give up.'

'Thanks, Dad. It's not easy, but it's worth it. I

remember when I first started in my new role in Lowestoft, I was nervous about being in a new town. But now, I seem to be settled.'

Keeley stared at Shenfield out of her window.

'I hardly recognise Shenfield now. There used to be shops there,' Keeley said pointing out of her window. 'Look, now it's all housing developments'.

Her Dad nodded as he focused on the road ahead.

'You remember your old school,' her Dad said as they drove past.

Memories resurfaced of her time at Shenfield High Academy. She thrived academically but found solace in a few close friends, particularly Jane Douglas, her constant companion during sixth form. They shared a special bond.

'Welcome back, Keels. Home sweet home,' her dad proclaimed as they pulled onto the driveway.

Keeley snapped back to the present, scanning her childhood home.

'Thanks, Dad. It's good to be home.'

'I'm sorry about what I said earlier, Keels. I didn't mean to upset you. I know that you are a police officer too. I'm proud of you.'

'It's okay. I know you're just trying to look out for me,' Keeley reassured him. 'I'm going to get an early night, Dad. Thanks for coming to get me.'

'Okay, dear, goodnight. Your old room is all set up for you,' he said with a warm smile.

Tiptoeing down the landing, Keeley entered

her childhood room. Band posters and school textbooks adorned the walls. Trophies and medals from cross-country running achievements lined the windowsill. Drawers and the wardrobe stood mostly empty, as her belongings had been relocated to Lowestoft.

Her eyes fell upon a photo on the windowsill —a picture of her and Jane. Memories of unrequited love flooded back, along with the sting of rejection. Keeley had kept her feelings hidden, even from her family. The fear of not being accepted loomed over her, a weight she carried silently.

Exhausted from the day's events, Keeley succumbed to sleep, her eyelids heavy with the weight of exhaustion.

<u>40</u>

After parking Angel, he walked up to the front door and knocked. He waited, the cool morning air made his breath visible in the dim light. Waiting patiently on the doorstep, he shrugged his shoulders and turned to head back to his car. Just as he took a step back, the door creaked open behind him.

'Hello, who is it?' the voice asked nervously, until they locked eyes with Cecil. 'Oh, it's you. Why are you here?'

'I think you know exactly why I'm here,' he replied.

'I'm not sure I understand what you mean,' she stammered.

Cecil held up the envelope, the printed note still inside. 'This arrived at my doorstep. Someone doesn't want me looking into Lizzie's death. I think you wrote this.'

'Mr Whitford, I'm... I'm afraid I don't know

what you're talking about,' she said, sheepishly avoiding eye contact. 'Now, if you don't mind, I'm getting ready to go out.' She attempted to close the front door but hesitated, clearly uneasy about the situation.

Cecil lunged forward and stuck his shoe in the door stopping it from closing.

'Mr Whitford, what do you think you are playing at? I will call the police if you do not go away!'

'I am happy to wait for them. Maybe then you can explain why I found one of your strawberry-blonde hairs stuck to the envelope this letter was sent in. I am sure they would be very interested.'

She seemed taken aback for a moment, then sighed, her shoulders slumping as if surrendering to the truth, as she opened the door again.

'Alright, Mr Whitford, you got me. I did send you that letter,' she admitted reluctantly.

He interrupted her before she could utter another word. 'You killed your sister. Why?' Cecil demanded.

Mrs Bardwell's eyes met his, a mix of sadness and regret in her eyes. 'No, Mr Whitford, not like that. I didn't kill her. I would never hurt my sister, I loved her.'

'Then why? Why send this note?' he demanded.

Mrs Bardwell hesitated, a tear escaping down her cheek. 'I just... I wanted you to stop. The allegations, the digging—I couldn't bear it. You turned up uninvited at her funeral and started putting all sorts of thoughts in my head. Wild ideas about someone wanting to murder my sister. I was a mess, unable to sleep and drowning my sorrows.'

Cecil's anger started to fade, giving way to a blend of pity and understanding. 'Mrs Bardwell, I didn't intend to cause you pain. I'm simply seeking the truth about what happened to Lizzie.'

'I know,' Mrs Bardwell whispered, wiping away her tears. 'But I can't handle the constant reminder of what we lost. I loved my sister and I can't let her memory be tainted by all of this. I need you to stop this pursuit.'

Cecil placed a gentle hand on her arm. 'Okay. I'll do my best to tread carefully, Mrs Bardwell. For both your sake and Lizzie's.'

He left the house feeling unsettled by the encounter. Mrs Bardwell's reaction had surprised him, a reminder that there was more to this mystery than met the eye. While she may not have been the culprit, he sensed that she was hiding something.

He slumped in his car seat, his breath coming in ragged gasps. The trail had gone cold, and he was starting to doubt whether he would ever find what he was looking for. He had been chasing this mystery for months, and it was taking its toll on him.

41

Her work alarm jolted her awake at 6 a.m. Eager to clear her mind, she retrieved her running gear and trainers from the closet.

Running through the neighbourhood, a sense of freedom washed over Keeley.

Her favourite playlist played in her ears, evoking nostalgia and encouraging her on.

Returning home, she entered the kitchen.

'Hi, there stranger. How was your run?' her mother asked. Her mother was seated at the kitchen table wearing her signature political bob and a tired expression.

Keeley felt a rush of emotions upon seeing her mother. She was happy to be reunited but nervous about the impending conversation.

'Mum, yeah, it was good. The weather's a bit chilly. How have you been?'

'Nothing to complain about. Well, except your father. Between us, he's driving me up the wall with his birdwatching obsession. Could you at least try to pretend to be interested, or better yet, go out with him while you're here? Maybe then he'll give up on me,' her mother said, a rare smile lighting up her face.

Keeley laughed.

'I've missed hearing that laugh around here,' her mother admitted warmly.

'How's work, Mum?' Keeley enquired, taking a seat at the table.

'Good. Have you heard? I've got a new job. I'm now leading anti-terrorism operations for the whole of London and the East of England.'

'Sounds exciting,' Keeley responded, impressed.

'How's it going with Lowestoft's finest?' her mother asked.

'Mum! Why do you always have to be so condescending?' Keeley snapped.

'I'm not? I just want the best for you. Don't you want to solve crimes that matter? Remember when we used to call you *Harriet the Spy*?' her mother said.

'I might consider that in the future, but now I want to make my own legacy. I don't want any favours. As a matter of fact, I'm working on something interesting.'

Keeley went on to share her recent experiences with Miss Hargrave and Miss Watson, tactfully avoiding the embarrassing incident with the bird smashing into the windscreen.

'Maybe it isn't as boring as I originally thought in Lowestoft. If it was me, my dear, I would not waste your time on this. I've encountered members of the public who think they're sleuths trying to solve fictional crimes. Mr Whitford sounds like that sort of person. What does your sergeant make of all this? What's his name again?' her mother asked.

'Parker. He's unsure and told me to ignore this. He's too stubborn to see that something is not right about these deaths.'

'Well, it sounds like it's settled then.'

Keeley sighed, 'Why do you have to be like this, Mum? I'm going to head upstairs and get ready. We'll talk later,' she said with a forced smile, rising from the table.

Her mother nodded, and Keeley left the kitchen, heading upstairs to shower and dress.

She headed back downstairs and went into the kitchen to make a hot drink. Her father had anticipated her readiness for coffee, for he was already pouring one for them both.

'Keels. Fancy a quick outing before you head back? How about Warley Place? We haven't been there in ages?'

'Yes, I've got time before my train later. I promise I will try and stay for longer next time.'

After drinking their coffees, they stepped out of the house and into the bright sunshine. Keeley couldn't help but feel a surge of excitement.

Bouncing along the rugged path in her dad's Jaguar, Keeley smiled, taking in the vibrant summer colours that adorned the surroundings.

'Ever seen a nuthatch?' her dad asked, grinning.

'Can't recall. What do they look like?' responded Keeley.

'Imagine a blue-grey bird with chestnut hues and a slender black stripe on its head. A plump woodpecker, smaller than a great tit,' her dad explained.

'Will we find those birds where we're headed?'

'Absolutely,' her dad replied.

'So, what's been going on with your recent encounters with your mother?'

Her dad knew of the often strained relationship between Keeley and her mum.

'You know how it is. Our conversations were a bit strained, but we did discuss her new role. It sounds pretty exciting.'

'She's resilient, your mother. Proud of you, even if she doesn't say it. With time, things will mend. She blames herself for pushing you away,' he confessed.

Keeley shook her head. 'Not her fault. I chose Lowestoft to escape Shenfield.'

Keeley's eyes drifted over the landscape.

Her dad cleared his throat, breaking the silence, 'Guess who I ran into recently?'

'No idea, who?'

'Trudy Douglas'

'Oh right. How are they doing?'

Memories of Jane's rejection flushed Keeley's cheeks—the moment that served as the catalyst for profound change. She hadn't told her dad about Jane's rejection, a silent part of her decision to leave Shenfield. It had become a painful reminder—an unrequited love she couldn't endure. Escaping became imperative—a chance to rediscover herself where judgement and rejection couldn't reach. And so she pursued a career in the police force—a fresh beginning where her past remained unknown.

'She was telling me Jane is engaged now. Do you two still speak?'

'Not anymore. We lost contact after I moved to Lowestoft,' Keeley replied.

She glanced out the car window at the passing landscape.

'Pity. You were close,' her dad said. 'Here we are!'

'You know, Dad, I've been cautious about discussing my personal life at work. It just simplifies things, especially being in the police force.'

Her dad nodded understandingly, his acceptance evident. 'I know it can be challenging, Keels. Your mother and I, well, we're different in some ways. I've always accepted you for who you are, but you know your mother, she's more traditional. It's been a bit more complicated for her.'

After hours of searching for wildlife,

including the nuthatch, to no avail, Keeley's dad drove her to the station.

'I'm sorry it's been a flying visit, got lots on at work at the moment. I promise to come for a few days next time. Thanks for today, it was good to get out. Hopefully, next time we will spot a nuthatch! I'll text you later when I get home.'

Collecting her bag, she closed the car door and entered the station. She scanned the timetables, searching for the train back to Lowestoft. As the train's departure was announced, part of her welcomed the return to her life in Lowestoft, where she had forged her own path and discovered a sense of purpose. Yet, a hint of nostalgia tugged at her heart, a gentle reminder of the bittersweet memories from her visits to Shenfield.

With a heartfelt sigh, she stepped onto the train, the doors closing behind her. She would have loved to stay longer, but with only a few days off, she had to return to the new life she had carved for herself.

__42__

PC Seddon strode purposefully towards her desk.

'Good break?' he asked.

'It was okay. Didn't do much, just went home for a few days to see my parents,' replied Keeley.

'Good to hear. Do you remember Alex Thompson?' said PC Seddon.

'Sierra's ex-boyfriend? I read your report. Why, what happened?'

'Wait until you see what I've just sent you.'

Keeley scanned her inbox and opened the single file attachment from Paul. A video started playing. Keeley leaned in, her focus on the screen. The grainy footage revealed Ipswich Hospital's Car Park F. People moved in and out of the shot, engrossed in their own worlds.

Keeled leaned in her focus on the screen, 'Sorry Paul, what am I looking for?'

'Patience, wait for it...' He raised his hand

slightly, his fingers trembling with anticipation. 'Any minute now...' And then, as the moment arrived, he couldn't contain his excitement any longer. 'Boom!' he exclaimed, clapping his hands together with a triumphant grin on his face.'

On the monitor, a familiar face emerged. Alex Thompson. He hung around the entrance, appearing inconspicuous.

Keeley checked the timestamp. 'Oh my god. This is the same night that Sierra ended her life!' Her eyes remained fixed as Alex's actions played out on screen.

PC Seddon nodded enthusiastically in response, then replied, 'I know, this cracks his alibi wide open.'

Alex paced back and forth, his eyes darting around the hospital car park. Then Sierra came into shot in her nurse's uniform, her body language immediately defensive. Keeley watched as they visibly began shouting at each other. Alex's body language grew aggressive, and he lunged forward, grabbing Sierra's arm. Sierra jerked away, her eyes wide with fear.

Sierra then managed to push him away, as she hastily got into her car. Alex then tried to open the driver's door and then slammed his fist down onto the bonnet.

Her terrified expression was captured by the security camera as she sped away.

Keeley rewound, watching the scene again.

'That little lying bugger,' Keeley muttered

under her breath.

Keeley closed her eyes and took a deep breath. This added complexity to the case. She suspected Alex originally, but his alibi cleared him at the time, whereas now the footage painted a darker picture.

She turned to PC Seddon, who was watching the footage with her. 'We need to question Thompson again,' she said firmly.

PC Seddon nodded seriously. 'Now we have this footage, it changes everything. Our suspicions are stronger now.'

Later that day, after a thorough discussion with Sergeant Parker, she obtained a warrant. Keeley didn't anticipate Sergeant Parker's willingness to assist, but with PC Seddon already requesting the footage, there seemed to be little room for argument when it ultimately proved to be inconsequential.

Keeley and PC Seddon were ready to apprehend Alex Thompson. They knew that the new evidence warranted his arrest.

43

Keeley felt a familiar sense of tension as they arrived at Alex's residence, parking their police vehicle down the road to avoid drawing attention.

She exchanged a determined glance with PC Seddon, both recognizing the importance of making a successful arrest. They knew they needed to handle this situation with precision as they both moved stealthily up the street towards the house.

Giving a subtle nod to PC Seddon, Keeley squared her shoulders and approached Alex's front door. The wood felt cold under her hand as she knocked firmly, each knock resonating with the weight of the moment. No answer.

Once more, she knocked forcefully on the door.

'Alright, I'm comin'! a voice yelled from the other side of the door.

Moments later, the door opened, and Alex appeared, his expression a mixture of surprise and unease.

'Mr Thompson,' Keeley stated in a calm and authoritative tone, 'we are here to inform you that you are under arrest for further questioning regarding the death of Sierra Watson.'

Alex's face went ghostly white and his words stuttered out in a mixture of shock and denial. 'Arrest? What the hell, I—I didn't... I've already told you everything I know!'

Keeley met his gaze, 'Mr Thompson, please cooperate and come with us.'

'Mr Thompson, you have the right to remain silent. Anything you say can and will be used against you in court. Put your hands behind your back so I can cuff you,' PC Seddon stated firmly.

Alex's eyes darted around the room, his face pale and his jaw clenched tight. Without warning, he lunged toward the door, trying to slam it shut.

PC Seddon's foot shot out, wedging itself in the doorway. Alex shoved against the door, but it held firm. The two men glared at each other, their muscles straining.

'Alex! You're making the situation very difficult. Stop this now!' yelled PC Seddon

Inside the house, Alex's panic intensified. 'Get the fuck outta ma house man, I'm warnin' ya!'

Alex launched a beer bottle at PC Seddon with all his might, shattering it against the wall with a loud crash. Glass shards flew in every direction, but PC Seddon continued to approach.

Keeley crept around the back of the house, her heart racing. She crouched between the parking garages and the neighbouring gardens, her ears straining for any sound. Inside the house, she could hear Alex shouting and the sound of crashing objects. She knew he was desperate to flee, and she was determined to stop him.

Alex overturned furniture and knocked objects aside, as he crashed through the rooms. PC Seddon edged closer, his eyes fixed on the suspect.

'Stop, Alex! There's nowhere left to run!'

Alex turned and fled through the back door, sprinting into the garden and out to the parking garages. He stopped momentarily, bent over, and began panting.

PC Seddon burst through the backdoor in pursuit.

Alex began to sprint again, when all of a sudden, he felt a powerful tackle from behind that knocked the wind out of him. He then felt a weight sit on top of him, pinning him to the ground.

Keeley looked down at him, her handcuffs drawn. 'You just had to do it the hard way,' she said.

She then grabbed his arms and locked his wrists behind his back.

Alex lay defeated beneath her, he cried out 'Get

the fuck off me! Ya bloody hurtin' me!'

Shortly after, they dragged him back to their police vehicle.

'I told you he would run,' PC Seddon said with a smirk.

'No way! You said he would run before he even opened the door,' Keeley replied.

With Alex's arrest completed, they headed back to the police station.

The flickering strip light in the interview room created an air of tension. Alex fidgeted in his seat, his eyes darting between Keeley and PC Seddon, who sat across from him.

Alex was read his rights and he sighed and shook his head.

Keeley took a deep breath, 'Mr Thompson, we need to address the recent developments in the Sierra Watson case. It has come to our attention that the alibi you provided during our initial investigation was not accurate. Lying to the police is a serious matter. We need to understand the reasons behind your false statement. Can you explain why you provided a misleading alibi?'

Alex shifted uncomfortably in his chair, a nervous glint in his eyes. 'I didn't exactly fib, I just... got a bit muddled up with the dates, you know? I was at my place that night, I swear.'

PC Seddon leaned forward slightly, maintaining his stern but professional demeanour. 'Mr Thompson, our investigation has uncovered evidence that contradicts your statement. We have CCTV footage that places you at a different location that evening. It's essential that you provide us with an accurate account of your whereabouts. Lying will only complicate matters further.'

'Nah, nah. I call bullshit! You got nothin',' Alex remarked confidently, shaking his head in response.

'We possess surveillance footage that places you in close proximity to Sierra's workplace on the night of her death,' Keeley declared firmly.

Surprise flashed across Alex's face, followed by an attempt to feign indifference as he shrugged his shoulders.

PC Seddon began tapping away on his laptop, then swivelled it around to face Alex, 'Well, what do you make of this?' he said as he played the CCTV footage.

Alex watched the video footage in front of him. As the video went on he wiped the sweat that had formed on his brow. Then pleadingly looked up towards the police officers, 'Nah, nah, it's not like that! Trust me,' he explained with a hint of desperation, 'I had absolutely no involvement in her death!'

'Mr Thompson,' Keeley said as she leaned forward, 'the surveillance footage captures what appears to be a heated argument between you and Sierra in the hospital's car park. We need you to explain that encounter.'

Alex swallowed hard, realising the seriousness

of the situation. 'Alright, alright, you got me,' he admitted with a sigh. 'Sierra and I 'ad a bit of a complicated history, you know? After her mum passed, I convinced her to nick some prescription drugs from the hospital. She was already on some and I thought we could make a few quid by takin' extra.'

Keeley and PC Seddon glanced at one another.

'What did you do with the drugs you stole?' Keeley enquired.

'Gave it to some blokes to flog. I'd get a piece of the action for providin' the stuff. They seemed to be from Europe, smugglin' it through Harwich and the Channel Tunnel.'

PC Seddon leaned in. 'Why did you confront her that night?'

Alex lowered his eyes and nodded solemnly. 'Yeah, I did. I'd left her be when we called it quits, but the blokes I was shiftin' the gear to, they started throwin' threats about breakin' my legs if I didn't start providin' 'em with more. I was bloody scared, thought maybe I could persuade Sierra to lend a hand again.'

Alex's shoulders slumped. After a pause, he said, 'You see, she chickened out when they nearly nabbed her at her job when we were together. I didn't fancy her losing her gig, so I had a word, told her to lay off.'

'Mr Thompson, did you threaten her during the argument?'

Alex sighed, his regret showing. 'Yeah, I lost it

and raised my voice. But I never meant to do her harm. I still had a soft spot for her, even with all the mess. I just wanted her to be safe, you know?'

'Mr Thompson, we need to uncover the truth. Did you have any involvement in Sierra's death?' asked Keeley.

Tears welled up in Alex's eyes. 'Nah, I'm telling ya straight, I had nothing to do with her death. After our argument, she drove off, and that was the last time I laid eyes on her.'

Keeley's lips curled into a triumphant smile as she stepped out of the interview room.

'I can't believe it. We did it!' Keeley exclaimed to PC Seddon.

'I'll pass Alex and the evidence onto the National Crime Agency to investigate the drug traffickers Alex had worked with. Good work today, Keeley!' said PC Seddon.

Keeley couldn't help but feel a surge of excitement amidst the intensity. It was moments like these that made her realise even the seemingly quiet town of Lowestoft held its share of hidden mysteries and dark secrets.

While she had been so confident that Alex was behind Sierra's death, the truth was more complex. This interview had ruled him out as a potential suspect, but another could still be at large.

44

Cecil's eyes searched Pakefield Road for the familiar dark green shop front of "Tulips" proudly displayed on a green awning above the florist shop. It had always struck him as an odd name for a florist, but he'd learned that tulips were a significant crop in Norfolk, not just in the Netherlands.

Cecil parked his vehicle and approached the front door only to see the "CLOSED" sign hung in the window.

He checked his pocket watch and saw that it should have been open. He liked to get there early and make sure everything was ready for the day. He had a list of tasks to do.

Cecil knocked firmly on the glass window.

Kay's eyes widened and she gasped, her red curls falling loose from her messy bun as she peered through the window blinds. Her glasses slipped down her nose. Her eyes darted around nervously.

She half-opened the door, her eyes wide and her lips trembling. She took a deep breath and pulled the corners of her mouth into a strained smile. 'Oh, blimey, it's you, Cecil! Thank the Lord for that. Sorry, Cecil, we're shut today,' she said.

'Kay, is everything okay?' he asked.

'Sorry, I'm a bit busy at the moment. Lots of flowers to arrange, you know. Could you pop by tomorrow instead?'

Cecil stopped the door from shutting. 'Kay, open the door,' he demanded.

As Kay opened the door, Cecil's eyes widened at the sight of a purple bruise on her right cheek. He felt a surge of concern and anger. 'Kay, what happened to you?' he asked.

Kay slammed the door shut and turned the key with a shaky hand. She peeked through the window blind.

'Well, Cecil, I've certainly seen better days.'

'I can see that. What happened there? That's a nasty-looking bruise.'

Kay instinctively touched the side of her face. 'Oh, it's nothing, just a clumsy mishap.'

Cecil simply nodded.

Kay after a few moments filled the awkward silence.

'Well, it all unfolded last night. I was just finishing up an order, and out of nowhere, there was a knock at the door. It must've been around 9 p.m., which, mind you, is rather late, but I've had customers show up at all sorts of odd hours to collect their orders. So, without checking first, I headed over to unlock the door. You see, the blind was already down at that point. And before I could even react, the door was pushed open with quite some force, smacking me right in the face and sending me tumbling to the ground.'

Cecil looked around the shop and saw scattered soil, broken pieces of a vase, and decapitated flower heads near the front door.

His brow furrowed as he processed Kay's words. 'Kay, oh my goodness! You poor thing. What happened next?'

'It all happened so suddenly. Two men barged in—one of them creating utter chaos while the other held a knife to my throat. They demanded that I open the till. I was petrified, utterly petrified, Cecil. I didn't know what to do.'

'Bless you, that is awful! What did the police say?'

'No! No police, Cecil! I'm quite serious, no involvement of the police, please! They warned me, and the very idea of bringing the police into this... well, it sends shivers down my spine. I want to avoid any further trouble if I can help it. I can manage without the money they took.'

'Okay, no police!'

'Promise me?'

Cecil raised his hand, crossing his fingers, and offered a sincere smile. His focus then shifted as he pointed up towards the CCTV camera that faced him. 'Does that work, Kay?' he said.

'Oh, that old contraption. It's been quite temperamental lately, especially with the video acting all peculiar. Another thing to add to my never-ending list, I suppose. You know, Cecil, it's just one thing after another. And what if there's another break-in? The insurance company would be absolutely livid,' Kay explained with a touch of frustration.

'Don't worry, Kay. I'll send Thomas over to take a look. He's good at fixing things.'

'Oh, Cecil, that would be ever so kind of you. How's he faring these days, staying out of mischief, I trust?'

'He's doing very well. In fact, he got into College recently. He's studying motor vehicles, and wants to work at *Lotus Cars* one day.'

'Oh, Cecil, what you've done with that lad is marvellous! But before we have a good old natter, let me dash off and grab Kenneth Jasper's funeral arrangements. Such a tragedy about Kenneth. I knew his sister from school. Please pass on my condolences to his family,' Kay said.

Cecil held the door open for Kay as she carefully placed the chrysanthemum cross in the boot of the hearse. He gently closed the boot and turned to face her. 'Thank you, Kay. Are you sure you'll be alright?'

'I'll manage, Cecil. No need to fret. Best of luck with the Jasper family. I hope the service brings them some comfort.'

He climbed into the driver's seat and started the engine. Looking back at Kay as she made her way back inside the shop, he wondered how long it would be before the robbers returned, and what they might do next.

Cecil drove slowly away, his mind racing. He knew he had to do something to protect Kay, but he didn't know what.

45

'The deceased is female, approximately twenty years old.' He lifted her chin and saw the dark bruises around her neck. 'Evidence indicates severe physical trauma, including signs of manual strangulation.' He then ran his fingers over the broken bones in her face, 'And blunt force injuries to the head,' said Dr Pilkington into the microphone.

He stopped the recording when someone knocked at the door.

'Come in.'

'Mornin', laddie! You're not still stuck tae this, are ye?' Dr Walsh spoke with a hint of a Glaswegian accent.

He clenched his jaw and forced a smile. 'Morning, sir,' he replied through gritted teeth. 'Just finished.'

'Took you long enough. What's the scoop?'

'I was just about to notify the coroner. You see,

it took longer as I found—'

'Always a stickler for the details, lad. Just remember, wed to your work, you'll never leave these walls.' Dr Walsh strode into the room and glanced at the unclothed body on the metal table with a sneer. 'Another junkie,' he muttered.

'Got it, sir. Need something?'

He checked his phone and frowned. 'I've got a tee time in ten minutes at Newton Green,' he said, grabbing his coat and hat. 'And then I've got to meet with those reporters about the Pinecone Case...'

'Impressive.'

'Anyway, I'm in a rush.' Dr Walsh glanced at his watch. 'Can I count on you to have a look at something?'

'Sure. You're the boss,' Dr Pilkington replied

'That's the spirit. Ipswich police left something for us yesterday evening. Unfortunately, I won't be able to get to it this morning. I've assigned the task to the new APT—can't recall his name, the lad with the blonde curls and a face marked by acne. Anyway, he's preparing it for you in the next room when you're done here. I need you to get your findings to the police quickly. They seem to believe it's urgent so be quick. Catch you later.'

'Okay, sir, leave it with me. Have a good—' Dr Pilkington sighed in frustration mid-sentence. '—And he's gone, just like that, the famous Dr Walsh.'

Dr Pilkington resumed speaking into his recording 'Traces of fentanyl, cocaine, and methamphetamine have been found in her system. This explains why the deceased shows no defensive wounds. We can rule this as first-degree murder.'

Dr Pilkington asked for help to store the body and samples. He grabbed new gloves and an apron from the closet and changed.

Stepping into the next room, he saw the new anatomical pathology technician arranging something on a table, his back turned.

'So, what's Dr Walsh got for us this morning?' Dr Pilkington's voice broke through the quiet, surprising the young APT as he spun around.

'Hey, Dr Pilkington! I'm Seb. I just started last week,' he said.

'Nice to meet you, Seb. What are we looking at?'

'This case is quite unusual, sir. I've not seen anything quite like it!"

Dr Pilkington studied Seb, 'Is that right?'

Seb stepped aside and revealed the gruesome sight on the table.

'Where's the rest?' Dr Pilkington asked.

'Yeah, that's all we've got. And what's interesting is the police found it beneath a home safe. Dr Walsh didn't bring that up?'

Dr Pilkington paused, shaking his head and wiping his brow as he studied the gruesome sight on the table. 'He's unbelievable! Clearly,

Dr Walsh left out some key details in the conversation we just had. Like, why do we only have what looks like mashed-up fingers?'

Seb nervously smiled in response.

Letting out a deep breath, Dr Pilkington forced a smile. 'I was thinking it would be another dull task from Dr Walsh. What's required?'

'The safe chopped off the thief's fingers. We need to get fingerprints from them to find out who they are.'

'Yes, sounds about right, Seb,' replied Dr Pilkington.

'Okay, have you analysed the fingers, if we can still call them that, for friction ridge skin on the tips?' Dr Pilkington asked.

Seb checked and said, 'Yes, they're intact.'

'Listen closely,' Dr Pilkington instructed. 'You'll collect DNA samples and fingerprints. Start with any remaining nail clippings for DNA evidence. For fingerprints, no live scan, so we'll use basic methods—ink and stock fingerprint cards. But before recording, dry the skin to reduce smudging.'

He guided Seb, explaining how to collect, seal, and prepare the fingers for examination. Then, he had Seb clean the table for the next task. Dr Pilkington left the room, shaking his head at the sight of the severed fingers. He wondered if he'd even want lunch—this day wouldn't be routine.

Mr Whitford's theories on the suicides and their similarities to his morning case added to Dr

Pilkington's stress.

46

Later in the day, Cecil drove the hearse down Blackheath Road, followed closely by several vehicles. Angel was not large enough to accommodate the entire Jasper family, so Cecil drove alone while the family travelled in the other hearse with his assistant, Thomas.

He had hired Thomas at the request of his mother, who was concerned about the company he was keeping. Cecil was happy for the help and it gave Thomas a chance to apply what he was learning in college to keep his old car running.

As they waited at the traffic lights, Cecil's eyelids drooped. He had been waking up at the crack of dawn for weeks, juggling the demands of multiple families. This morning, he had meticulously prepared for the funeral service, coordinating with the family and ensuring every detail was perfect, from the flowers to the music. Yet, despite his exhaustion, he felt a sense of calm confidence that everything was ready.

Cecil flicked his eyes to the rearview mirror, where he saw Thomas's hearse with the Jasper family trailing him. He eased off the accelerator pedal and flashed his brake lights, hoping they would catch up as he reached some roadworks, where a sign said, "One lane ahead". He waited for the green light and then moved on, hoping the traffic wouldn't delay them too much. He glanced in the mirror again, but this time he couldn't see the other hearse. He frowned and wondered if they had been stuck at the red light. He trusted that Thomas knew the way to the cemetery.

The hearse continued along the road until it reached Kirkley Cemetery. Cecil drove through the lychgate and past the Twin Chapels, with the old oak tree serving as his marker for the planned grave location. As he parked, he noticed cars parking wherever space allowed as additional mourners began to arrive.

Six men in black suits lifted the coffin from the hearse and carried it with solemn steps to the grave. They set it down gently on the straps that would lower it into the earth. Mourners gathered around the grave, their hushed tones and tears filling the air. The coffin was lowered into the ground as a short, round-faced priest began delivering the eulogy in a deep voice.

Cecil noticed that his assistant Thomas and the rest of the Jasper family were still missing.

A loud shout cut off the priest's eulogy, making everyone turn their heads.

'What? That's not right! His name is Gareth, Father?' A man in a blue shirt stood up and pointed at the coffin.

Another man in a grey suit joined him. 'What are you on about? My uncle was called Kenneth!'

The priest tried to quiet them down, asserting, 'Excuse me, you're being disrespectful to the family gathered here today. I'm trying to give a eulogy.'

Cecil heard Thomas's voice and turned to see the other car parked in the distance. The Jasper family emerged from the back seats.

Sorry we're late, Mr Whitford. You'll never guess what happened! We followed the wrong hearse to another funeral. Bloody roadworks on London Road South!

Cecil smiled to himself, but before he could say anything, his attention was drawn back to the crowd.

In a sudden turn of events, one of the men sprinted towards the priest, grabbing his thin black tippet scarf. The priest swiftly retaliated, landing a well-placed punch that sent the man stumbling backwards. The man lost his balance and fell into the hole that had just been prepared for the casket.

A small group of people ran to the edge of the grave and peered down. Two of the men climbed down and helped the man to his feet. Then lifted him out of the grave and deposited him on the ground.

Once the eulogy concluded, a handful of dirt was dropped onto the casket lid.

The wail of a siren and the flashing lights signalled the arrival of a police vehicle at the cemetery entrance. Two officers approached the gathering.

'We received a call about fighting and disturbance complaints. Can someone explain what's going on?' asked one of the officers.

Cecil, recognising a familiar face among the officers, stepped forward. 'I can explain, officer. We were en route to the funeral but got caught in roadworks. Some of our party mistakenly followed the wrong hearse to another funeral, and it seems we unintentionally picked up a few attendees from that service. This funeral is for a man named Kenneth Jasper.'

One of the men near the unconscious body exclaimed, 'Oh, shit!'

After gathering statements and conversing with all parties involved, the police officers defused the situation. The man who had been knocked down decided not to press charges against the priest and was escorted away by his friends, presumably heading to the correct cemetery.

Most of the mourners had started to depart and the commotion had finally settled.

'Why are you always where the trouble is, Mr

Whitford?' Keeley asked.

Cecil chuckled softly. 'It seems like trouble has a way of finding me, PC Cooper.'

As she wrapped up her conversation with Mr Whitford, Keeley looked around the churchyard and remembered the incident at Lizzie's funeral, where James and Rob had clashed.

She remembered Rob mentioning during the interview that James was a violent person and had even threatened to kill him. Rob being behind Lizzie and Sierra's deaths still did not sit right with her.

47

He heard stock car engines in his head as he sat in his mother's Golf. He missed those weekends at King's Lynn Stadium with his father, a stock car champion.

His father died of lung cancer when he was fifteen and his life changed. School became a distraction, and caring for his grieving mother grew increasingly difficult. Inevitably, he fell in with a rough crowd that cared more about nights out and causing mischief than his future. The threat of expulsion loomed over him, a result of his truancy and run-ins with the police.

Months passed, and he hadn't seen Mr Whitford since his father's funeral. He remembered the serious-looking funeral director, a man of few words but immense poise. It was surreal when he saw him again, picking him up in a hearse after a night out with friends—a night that marked the end of many friendships.

As they drove in silence, Mr Whitford's presence was strangely comforting. The older man had shared the pain of losing his own father to cancer and steered the conversation toward Thomas's passions, particularly motorsports. He discovered that his mother had orchestrated the meeting, hoping Mr Whitford's influence would help him. It did.

The following day, Mr Whitford introduced Thomas to a friend from his Royal Navy days, a director at *Lotus Cars*. A tour of the factory and the director's passionate talk about career opportunities rekindled his desire to excel. He returned to school with newfound determination, achieving the grades needed for college.

Mr Whitford had once helped Thomas and his mother, so Thomas felt obligated to return the favour.

As he drove down London Road South, his mind wandered back to the time his father taught him to drive, taking rides around the industrial estate. The thrill of manoeuvring the car through those early lessons brought a smile to his face.

After parking in front of the flower shop, Thomas felt a surge of satisfaction as he glanced back at his car, the green "P" sign glistened proudly, a symbol of his hard-earned driver's licence. It was a small emblem that showed his resolve and, he felt, it was a connection to his father.

He entered the flower shop and smelled the flowers. Kay was talking to a customer by the orchids. He had learned a lot about flowers from Mr Whitford. This experience had not only taught him the value of hard work but also an appreciation for life and its fleeting nature. While working at the funeral home was not something he had initially imagined he would enjoy, his first funeral reminded him of his own experience of loss and the impact that support from others can have during such difficult times.

'Hello there, Thomas, my dear!' Kay exclaimed, spreading her arms wide, ready for a warm embrace. Her smile was a beacon of genuine joy. 'It's an absolute delight to see you! How's your dear mother these days?'

Thomas gave her a hug but gently corrected her, saying, 'Hey, Kay, it's Tom. Not Thomas.' He couldn't help but grin. Kay was such a sweetheart, and her little mix-ups were always cute. 'Only my mum and Mr Whitford call me that. Yeah, my mum's doing well, thanks for asking. Mr Whitford mentioned you had some trouble the other night. Are you okay?'

Kay stopped smiling and looked worried.

'Oh, it was absolutely dreadful, but I'm on the mend now. How did today's service go for the Jasper family?'

'Well, it was pretty eventful, you know? There

was some mix-up with another funeral, and the wrong family ended up at the Jaspers'. Things got crazy, as you can imagine.'

'Oh my, that sounds like quite the conundrum, doesn't it? Right then, lots to take care of. Follow me, dear. I had this system installed years ago, but I've never quite figured out how to work it.'

'Sure thing. Let me take a look, see if I can sort it out.'

Thomas followed Kay to a messy storage room. She showed him the computer monitor with the shop's security system. Kay, somewhat awkwardly, manoeuvred the computer and logged in, revealing three flickering squares on the screen. Unfortunately, the image of the shop's interior, which he had just walked through, was hard to see because it was blurry and unclear.

'You see, it's in a right state! You can hardly make out a thing,' said Kay.

'Let me check it out. You got a manual for this thing?'

She handed Thomas a white, A4-sized, stapled series of pages with the same logo and company name on the front. 'I'll be out front if you need me. Don't worry if you can't sort it out. I can try to find the company that installed it and call them tomorrow if need be.'

Thomas checked the manual but discovered it only covered installation and setup. He turned to his phone, searched for the security system's make and model online, and found helpful troubleshooting videos. The first video, presented by a middle-aged security professional, lasted ten minutes. After watching it and adjusting the settings, Thomas improved the camera's image quality.

After setting up the DVR and cables, he eagerly delved into reviewing the events from the previous night. He accessed the programme, navigated to the "History" section, and began scrolling back to the evening before. In the footage, he observed Kay's busy florist routine, skilfully arranging and packaging flowers with evident passion.

Thomas saw how Kay's attention then shifted to the shop's entrance. As she moved to open the door, it was abruptly thrust open, causing her to stumble backwards and collide with a display stand, knocking over several pots. Two men, their faces half-concealed by snoods and caps, entered the shop. In shock, he witnessed one of them grabbing Kay's apron and dragging her toward the till. The sight of the knife made Thomas shiver.

He strained to see what happened next as Kay was pushed aside and the man began to grab a stack of notes, stuffing them into his jacket pocket. While the robber's face was hard to make out, he was sure he recognised one of them, someone he hadn't seen in years. His heart pounded in his chest, and his palms were sweaty.

He felt like he was going to throw up.

'How's it going for you, my dear? Have you managed to sort it out?'

'Um... one sec.' He quickly closed the window and returned to the live view of the shop. 'Yeah, all done.'

'Oh, you clever young man. It's good to know we have a tech-savvy youngster around to assist an old lady like me. To express my gratitude, I've arranged a bouquet of lovely pink roses and scented oriental lilies, with a sprinkle of gypsophila, for your mother.'

'No problem at all, Kay. I reckon she'll love 'em. Just hit me up if it starts acting up again, alright?'

'Thank you once more. Please let Cecil know that the order for the funeral on Friday will be ready for pickup tomorrow.'

'Got it. It's odd hearing you call him by his first name like that. Not many folks call him Cecil.'

She smiled at him. 'He's an odd one, isn't he? But there's a certain charm to him, something so noble and endearing lurking beneath that chilly exterior, once you get to know him.'

'Yeah, defo! He's a real good one. Helped me and my mum out a ton. I've gotta make tracks. Loads of coursework to catch up on. Spending the day at the Jaspers' has put me a bit behind, you know how it is.'

After leaving the shop, he made his way back to his car. During the drive home, he found it hard to shake off what he had witnessed on the CCTV footage. Uncertainty gnawed at him about how to proceed with this newfound information. Given his limited trust in people, he held the belief that Mr Whitford would know what to do. Ever since his father's passing, he had grown to appreciate the support he had received from him.

Yes, Mr Whitford would know how to handle the situation.

48

Nestled into his well-worn armchair, a well-thumbed copy of "*Treasure Island*" in his hands, Cecil read through the cherished pages of his childhood books with nostalgia. He remembered how he used to dream of joining the Royal Navy and living a life like a pirate. He sighed and shook his head, amused by his childish fantasies. How different they were from the harsh realities of modern piracy that he had faced as a naval officer. Buccaneers with peg legs, eye patches, or menacing hooks for hands just simply didn't exist. Instead, the pirates he crossed paths with in the Gulf of Aden bore darker skin tones and obscured their faces with bandanas. They were armed with assault rifles and rocket-propelled grenade launchers.

Cecil's concentration was broken by the jarring sound of knocking at the front door.

He checked the time. It was late. He wasn't

expecting anyone. He got up, turned off the light, and crept down the hall. He saw a shadow move outside the door.

Before reaching the front door, he passed into the welcoming front room, a space intended for comforting bereaved families. Approaching the window, he gently shifted the curtain aside, peering through the gap to catch a glimpse of who was outside. Relief washed over him as he recognized Thomas.

Thomas's hands fidgeted with his jacket zip and his eyes darted around the room.

Cecil could sense the tension in Thomas's body, and he knew that something was wrong.

He walked towards the front door and unlocked it.

As he opened the door, 'Sorry, Mr Whitford! I know it's kinda late, but, you see, I don't know what to do.' His words rushed out in a frantic tumble.

'Slow down, Thomas. Why don't you come on in and tell me what's troubling you?' Cecil widened the door to usher Thomas inside before closing it behind him.

'Come through to the office; I'm set up there this evening.'

He trailed Thomas into his office, a space overflowing with books where he had been engrossed in his reading.

'It seems like something is bothering you, Thomas. How about you tell me what's troubling you before you create crop circles on the carpet?'

'I'm not sure what to do. You're always good at handling tough stuff. But, man, forget it. This is, like, totally different. I don't even know why I'm telling you this. It's hopeless, nothing we can do,' Thomas said.

Cecil leaned in and offered a reassuring smile. 'Thomas, I understand the weight of difficult situations. I've got a knack for handling things, but if you're here, it's worth discussing. So, why don't you share what's on your mind? Perhaps, together, we can shed some light on this seemingly insurmountable situation.'

'I did that thing you told me to, went to Tulips earlier to fix the CCTV stuff. It's all sorted now. But, man, I couldn't help myself. I peeked at the footage from the break-in. You won't believe it, but I think I might've actually recognised one of the attackers!'

Cecil stood there silently, his hands folded behind his back, patiently waiting for Thomas to continue.

'Um, it's, like, someone I used to hang with a while back. His name's Frank Edmunds. He's a real bad guy! I used to hang out with him; he's a few years older than me. Most of us were scared of him. I heard he was charged with assault for beating up another guy pretty badly years ago. The guy needed stitches and surgery for, like, a busted retina or something. But, you know, they dropped the charges in youth court, probably 'cause he threatened the other guy or something. Anyway, from the video, I'm dead certain it was him pulling off the Tulips job the other night. So, what's our move here? I don't wanna get the police involved. I'm worried about Kay and my mum. I left all that craziness behind, and I don't want them caught up in any mess.'

'Thank you for bringing this to my attention, Thomas. You did the right thing by sharing this information with me. I agree that it's a difficult situation,' he replied thoughtfully. 'If this young man isn't afraid of the law, we need to take matters into our own hands. Do you know where I can find him? I may need to pay him a visit.'

'What! Nah, that is a seriously bad idea, Mr Whitford,' Thomas replied, concern etched on his face. 'You can't seriously be thinking about confronting a dangerous man like him! I get that you're brave and all that, but that would be a really stupid idea!'

'Perhaps. Though I can be quite persuasive when I need to be,' Cecil replied calmly. 'You know me better than most, Thomas. I live by rules and discipline, and I don't back down from a fight when the people I care about are in danger. Don't worry, I'll be careful.'

Thomas felt uneasy and avoided making eye contact with Cecil. 'Well, I haven't seen him in ages. I did attend a sick house party he hosted once. I think it was at 22 Dene Road.'

Cecil walked across to his desk and scribbled

the address down on a notepad.

'Remember, he's bad news, so be careful. I must be on my way, I have college in the morning. Also, before I forget, Kay said Friday's flowers are ready for collection tomorrow.'

He closed the door behind Thomas and settled back into his armchair, reaching for his copy of *"Treasure Island."* He looked at the front cover, drawing parallels between the swashbuckling tale and the unsettling situation involving Frank Edmunds.

Cecil thought about how those who were greedy and made bad choices deserved to be punished, unfortunately the right adversary never steps in. Restless with these thoughts, he set the book aside and made his way over to his computer.

Moments later, he clicked the print button after double-checking the address one last time, ensuring there were no mistakes. He couldn't afford any errors, not with what he was about to do. The old printer in the corner of the room hummed to life, its creaky gears and worn-out rollers struggling to keep up. It chugged and screeched, ka-thunking, as it printed out the directions to 22 Dene Road.

Finally, the printer spat out a single sheet and he snatched it up, reviewing it once again. The address was correct, and the directions were clear. He knew exactly where he needed to go. He scanned the house for anything he could use, his eyes darting from the kitchen to the garage to the shed, stuffing each item into a backpack.

It wasn't much, but it would have to suffice for the task he had planned. He took a deep breath and hefted the backpack onto his shoulders. He left his house and stepped into the night.

49

Heading toward the address, he mentally reviewed the plan one last time, drawing on his well-practised tactical skills. His hands trembled slightly as he attempted to steady them; there was no turning back at this point. He couldn't ignore the unsteadiness, a stark contrast to the unwavering precision of his youth. Age had its way of reminding him that even the most reliable parts could falter over time.

He drove east on Denmark Road, following the directions. The drive was meant to take five minutes but his unfamiliarity with the area led him to proceed cautiously. As he navigated the turns and intersections, his mind raced with the knowledge that he had to do this. Those he cared for had already been hurt, and others were still at risk.

While driving down the road, he noticed a small group outside on the street he knew he would have to deal with first. To avoid arousing suspicion, he parked in a spot that offered a clear view of both the house and the gathering crowd, but far enough away so as not to disturb the scene.

The gathering consisted of six young men and three young women of similar age. The house, a red-brick terraced one, had its front door left open. Despite the closed car windows, he could hear the loud music thumping from within—a steady rhythmic beat with muffled rap lyrics. People were arriving and departing, with drinks and cigarettes in hand. This had to be the right location; Thomas had mentioned attending a house party at this very address.

He studied the house, drawing on his military training to assess its layout. He mentally noted three or four rooms branching off from a central landing and a single staircase in the main hallway.

Surveying the items he had brought along, he gathered them and exited his car.

Approaching the house, he halted beside a telegraph pole and covertly affixed a disc-shaped object to it using a nail. He carefully slipped it through the mounting hole to avoid drawing any notice.

Next retrieving a box of matches from his pocket, he ignited one against the rough surface, producing a small flame. Carefully, he set fire to the fuse, aware that time was limited before chaos would erupt. In his prime, he might have climbed the fence or taken a bolder route to avoid being noticed. Now, he needed to depend on a more straightforward strategy, one that his experience and cleverness could execute.

As he approached the house, a young man wearing a thick gold chain around his neck swaggered towards him, fists clenched and chest puffed out.

'Hey, old man, out this late? You'll need to pay for protection around here. Not safe for someone like you,' he jeered, snickering and gesturing towards his friends. 'Look at this clown, wearin' a bloody bow tie!'

Cecil glanced at his pocket watch, his brow furrowing. He knew time was running out but he didn't want to start a fight before reaching the house. He took a deep breath and tried to calm his racing heart.

He fixed the young man with a steely look, his expression hardening.

The young man's face flushed with anger and his fists clenched in response. 'Got ourselves an 'ard man here, lads!'

He stepped towards Cecil, but then stopped. Something froze him on the spot—a piercing intensity that seemed to penetrate through him. For a moment, he felt as though he was being scrutinised and assessed.

After several uncomfortable seconds, one of the young women called out, 'Tony, what ya playin' at? Just leave that poor man alone already. He's harmless.'

'Oh geez, Tony, you just got called out... such a tough man, picking fights with pensioners,' one of the other young men chimed in.

The young man smirked at Cecil and rolled his eyes. 'Fine, I was just messin'. No drama. Laters.' He sauntered back to his group, his shoulders swaying confidently.

Upon nearing the house, Cecil noticed a burly young man stationed by the doorway. Suddenly, a loud screech echoed, accompanied by bursts of vibrant flashes from the activated Catherine wheel.

'Hey, what the hell! Look over there, guys. It's not fireworks night!' one of the boys exclaimed.

With the group's attention diverted, Cecil swiftly redirected his focus to the front door. He watched as the young man who had stood guard entered the house. This was concerning; it implied the person was either reckless or fearless, both qualities making him a formidable opponent.

Upon entering the narrow hallway, the blaring music and the overwhelming scent of alcohol and smoke enveloped him. The young man he'd spotted earlier noticed and positioned himself to block the path.

Cecil took a deep breath and squared his shoulders. He had been in dangerous situations like this before, and he knew how to handle them. His experience as a Navy medic had taught him how to de-escalate conflicts and maintain a steady calm under pressure. He drew on his knowledge to defuse the potentially volatile situation ahead.

The young man stepped forward, his fists clenched and his jaw clenched. 'Whoa, hold on there, buddy. Private party. You better leave, old man.' His voice was barely audible through the pounding music.

Cecil threw up a calming hand gesture. 'No trouble here.'

The lad sneered. 'Yeah, well what ya doin' here? Get lost, grandad!'

'I'm searching for someone... Frank Edmunds. Is he here?' Cecil enquired.

'Nah, man... You gotta step aside. No Frank here,' the young bloke shot back.

Cecil's eyes narrowed and an eyebrow was raised. 'Are you absolutely certain? I have a strong reason to believe this is his house.'

The young lad just shrugged, that cheeky smirk still on his face. 'Believe what you want, old-timer, but Frank ain't around. Now sod off before I do it for ya.'

He took a step closer to the young man, his voice steely. 'I simply wish to have a brief conversation with him. I suggest you step aside.'

He hesitated for a moment, then shifted into a sumo-wrestler stance, poised to charge.

With a firm grip on the concealed hammer,

Cecil calmly and deliberately swung at the young man's thigh as he charged. The young man crumpled to the ground, his hostile expression morphing into pure terror as he looked up at Cecil.

'Ow! My leg! You've messed it up, man!' the young man whined.

Cecil moved quickly, lowering himself and pinning the young man with one knee, covering his mouth with a firm hand.

The young man's eyes widened in fear

Cecil leaned in close, his voice cold. 'Listen up and listen well. Your leg will heal, the impact has only crushed your femur, you've only fractured it so quit whining. I'm not here for you, tell me what I need to know and no further harm will come to you. Got it?'

He nodded in agreement.

'Good. Where's Frank?' he asked calmly.

The young man whimpered in pain. 'He's upstairs... in the first room on the left,' he said.

'Is anyone else in the house?' Cecil asked.

The young man shook his head. 'Just Frank and his girlfriend.'

Cecil delivered a firm backhand strike to the side of the young man's neck, causing him to grow dizzy and eventually lose consciousness.

Locating the main electrical panel beneath the stairs and turning off all the switches, he cast the house into complete darkness.

A moment later, an irate voice from upstairs

called down, 'Kiel! Oi, you bellend! You there, man? The lights are gone!'

Knowing he had limited time to act, Cecil quickly and quietly ascended the stairs and positioned himself outside the door the yelling was coming from.

'Oi, Kiel, you got your ears on? What you doin' out there?' The voice shouted again, and the bedroom door slowly creaked open.

Cecil gave the door a hard kick, causing it to swing wide open.

'Argh!... My face!'

Stepping into the room, he shone his flashlight around. He spotted a girl in the bed who had pulled the covers up and a man on his knees clutching his face.

'On your feet, Frank.'

Frank staggered to his feet, his nose bleeding heavily. He wiped the blood away with the back of his hand and glared at Cecil with hatred in his eyes. His fists were clenched at his sides, and his jaw was clenched. The girl in the bed sat up, her eyes wide with fear. She looked around the room, confused and disoriented. Cecil scanned the room with his flashlight, noting the dishevelled bed, empty beer bottles, and the persistent scent of marijuana.

'Take a seat and listen to me, Frank.'

'You've bloody smashed my nose, you... you wanker! I'm gonna... gonna knock you out, old man!'

Frank yelled in pain, collapsing to his knees and clutching his bleeding nose.

'Now, Frank, we seem to be having a bit of a misunderstanding here. Let's give this another try, shall we? I won't be so polite about it next time.' He paused, letting the threat sink in, before continuing. 'I'm here because the other day, there was a little incident involving you at a florist shop named Tulips. It caused quite a bit of trouble for someone close to me. You see, when someone endangers someone I care about, they experience my wrath.'

'What?! Nah, man... I ain't got a clue what you're on about, it wasn't me, old man.'

Cecil raised the hammer above his head again and Frank threw both hands up defensively.

'Alright, alright, maybe I've got a clue or two. Yeah, the joint on Pakefield Road, that one? Yeah, me and Kiel had a rummage. Needed some dough, mate. I can cough up what I nicked and a bit more! We've had a few dodgy gigs recently. Look over there—wads of cash. Grab the lot!'

Cecil shone his flashlight around the room, highlighting the disordered trail in the direction he was pointed. A considerable stack of bills and valuable-looking jewellery appeared out of place on the bedside table. Cecil cautiously made his way across the creaking floorboards, his eyes scanning the room for any potential threats. He reached the table and picked up the stack of notes. He counted the money quickly and pocketed it.

Checking his pocket watch, he knew he had to hasten his actions before those outside returned to the house.

Turning around, he felt a weight in his other pocket and remembered the digital voice recorder he had with him. He often used it to record arrangements and notes at the funeral home. He pulled it out of his pocket and pressed the red stop button. The spinning cassette within the recorder came to a whirling halt.

'This money, Frank, is restitution for what you've stolen, along with the emotional distress you've inflicted on my dear friend. Listen closely. You've inadvertently confessed to a rather serious crime on this tape, and I already have you captured on CCTV during your ill-advised escapade at the flower shop. If, by some unfortunate chance, you decide to come within a hundred metres of that charming little establishment again, I shall feel compelled to forward this recording to my trusted police contact. She possesses a certain, shall we say, tenacity that surpasses even my own. And I'm quite certain you'd rather avoid the less pleasant aspects of jail. I daresay a nice pretty boy like you might find it rather disheartening. Now, you two have a pleasant evening. I do hope our paths never cross again.'

Heading back down the stairs, Cecil moved cautiously, stepping over Kiel's unconscious body sprawled in the hallway. He halted, staring down at the young man with a twinge of empathy. It was clear that Kiel was little more than a pawn in Frank's treacherous game. Cecil couldn't help but ponder what series of unfortunate events had driven Kiel into a life of crime and violence. It made him reflect on Thomas and wonder if, without his intervention, Thomas might have faced a similar fate.

He paused, realising for the first time that several fingers were missing from his right hand and pondered the events that had led to such an injury.

Stepping out into the cool night, he observed that the group had dispersed down the street. Oblivious to the cessation of music and the house's darkness, they were engrossed in laughter and boisterous chatter where he had ignited the Catherine wheel. He ignored them and made his way to his car, his mind absorbed by the recent events.

'You still up and about, old man?' The young guy who'd first had a go at him sneered. 'Must be past your bedtime.'

Cecil smiled in response. He couldn't help but feel a sense of sadness for the young man and the others he had encountered tonight, trapped in a cycle of crime and violence.

He knew he had made his point, and he had seen the fear in Frank's eyes. Frank wouldn't pose a problem again. Nonetheless, youngsters these days engage in some reckless behaviour, he thought as he drove away.

<u>50</u>

Keeley slumped at her desk, rubbing her eyes. Seeing Mr Whitford had caused images of Lizzie and Sierra's lifeless bodies lying in the back of Mr Whitford's hearse to flash through her mind all night.

She was still deeply troubled by the unanswered questions about their suicides. Despite her mother and Sergeant Parker urging her to move on, she couldn't stop the persistent feeling that there was more to their deaths than appeared at first glance.

The phone rang, startling Keeley. She picked it up and answered in her professional voice. 'Good morning, Lowestoft Police Station, PC Cooper speaking. How may I help?'

The woman's nervous voice betrayed her nervousness. 'Oh, hello there, PC Cooper. Yes, yes, I'm calling you back, you see. I do apologise for the delay, but I've just come back from my holiday, you know. Oh, it was quite lovely, I must say. I went to that little seaside town with the charming ice cream parlour on the corner. My dear friend, Margaret, well, she swears by their butterscotch swirl. You see, we used to go there every summer back when we were... oh, what was I saying? Right, your call. I'm ever so sorry, dear.'

'Hi, sorry, who is this?'

'Well, you see, I'm Lizzie Hargrave's neighbour.' the caller said. 'Or, I should say, I was her neighbour. It's just that, well, it's quite a shock to me that she's no longer with us. I'm Diane Jones, by the way.'

Keeley searched her desk and drawers for a pen and notepad. 'Oh, yes! Thanks for calling me back, Mrs Jones. I just had a few questions about the night of Lizzie's death. According to her sister, you called her complaining of banging noises.'

'Yes, let me see now. Well, I was settled in for the night. You see it was a Sunday as I was watching an episode of Antiques Roadshow, I just love that show, never miss it. It was quite a good one, a young girl had a small brooch that had been a family heirloom. Oh, my goodness, I can't believe I'm telling you this, sorry. So there I was watching the television, when I heard shouting and the thudding of her front door,' Mrs Jones said. 'Now, I am not one of those nosy neighbours, but I was quite worried, so I went to the window.' She paused, taking a deep breath. 'Oh, my goodness, I just remembered now. I was watching the episode with the pearl necklace. It was exciting!'

'Mrs Jones, can you tell me what you saw outside please?'

'I couldn't see much, but I saw a man banging her door and continuing to shout. Then her door opened, and he went inside. Odd really.

'Did you see Rob banging on the door and shouting?'

'Rob? Her ex-boyfriend, Rob? It's funny you mentioned it now, yes, I did see him. He came earlier, but Lizzie didn't let him in. Now, as for the other man, I've bumped into him before, but I can't quite put a name to his face, if you catch my drift. I didn't know what to do, so I tried calling her sister, but she didn't answer.' She paused again, her voice catching in her throat. 'I know now, I probably should have called the police. I didn't know what to do.'

'Thanks, this is very helpful. Would it be possible for you to come to the station? I'd like to show you some pictures to see if you recognise the person you saw.'

'Oh, I could come at... well, no, that wouldn't quite work because I've got that appointment at the optician's, you see. But how about 1 p.m.? Oh, wait, scratch that, that's when the window cleaner's due. Hang on just a moment, dear, let me grab my diary.'

Keeley sighed and lowered her head onto her desk.

'Hello, are you still there, officer?' she asked. 'Oh, it says here, the window cleaner isn't coming today after all. I've got him scheduled for Monday, you see. So, should I plan to pop down at 1 p.m.?'

Keeley thanked her and ended the call. This new information was intriguing. Who was banging on Lizzie's door? Initially, she thought it was her ex-boyfriend, but now she discovered that he had visited earlier. Perhaps Lizzie had a secret lover like Sierra, someone her sister Lisa didn't know about.

The rest of her morning was relatively uneventful.

As Keeley enjoyed her sandwich at her desk, she spotted PC Seddon ambling over towards her, a harried expression on his face, escorting a peculiarly dressed older woman who sported a wild mane of curly, salt-and-pepper hair that refused to be tamed. The woman was mid-sentence, prattling on about something utterly trivial, and PC Seddon's expression showed that he needed help.

Keeley rose from her seat and met them halfway.

Thank you for coming, Mrs Jones,' Keeley greeted her warmly. 'Please, follow me this way.' She led Mrs Jones to her desk and pulled over a chair.

Diane settled into the chair with a slightly nervous smile, her eyes flitting around the police station's surroundings. 'You know, officer. Sat here, it's just like those murder dramas I love to watch on the telly. All those detectives with their complicated cases to solve.'

She chuckled softly, her fingers playing with the eclectic assortment of bracelets adorning her wrist. 'Never thought I'd find myself in the middle of one of those, though. Life certainly has its surprises, doesn't it?' She leaned forward, her oversized glasses perched precariously on her nose. 'But I suppose we must get on with it, right?'

'You're absolutely right, Mrs Jones,' Keeley replied. 'Life does have a way of surprising us when we least expect it. But that's what keeps things interesting, isn't it?' 'Keeley leaned in closer, 'And you know, real-life cases can be just as intriguing as those murder dramas on TV. Now, let's see if we can't solve this mystery together, just like they do on the telly.' Sliding across the desk several photographs, Keeley said 'I have a few photos I would like you to look at. See if you recognise any of them as the man you saw recently at Lizzie's house on the night she died?'

Mrs Jones began scanning through each photograph ever so slowly until she stopped on one.

'Have you found one you recognise?'

'Yes, this one. It's rather amusing, actually. He looks remarkably like my old butcher, Ralph Gibbons. A delightful chap, he always saved the juiciest cuts of beef. But, you see, when I acquired my dentures, I had to bid Ralph's shop goodbye; the meat was just too tough for my new set. Such a shame. I wonder what he is up to now. I'll have to pop in and say hello to him when I next pass by.'

'That's quite an interesting story, Mrs Jones. Let's stay focused on the photos, shall we?'

'Yes, the photos, of course dear. Now where were we? Let me see, nope, nope,' she said as she placed the final photograph on the desk. 'Sorry, officer, none of these was the man I saw. But you know, I did get a photo of him on my phone.'

Keeley leaned forward in her chair. 'Fantastic,' she said. 'I'd love to see that.'

'Yes, well, how do I work this now? My daughter, bless her heart, insisted I needed one of these contraptions. Said it was high time I joined the modern world. Oh, but they can be such confusing things for an old soul like me. But here we are, trying to make sense of it all,' she exclaimed as she gingerly slid the phone across the desk to Keeley.

Keeley examined the photo. The image was blurry and showed only a partial view of the man's face. However, there was something familiar about him. She tapped away on her computer. After a few minutes of searching,

Keeley sighed in frustration. 'Damn it, he's not in the database,' she said.

Taking a deep breath, she looked up at Mrs Jones. 'Thank you for your assistance, Mrs Jones. We'll keep working on this. If you remember anything else or come across any other information, please don't hesitate to reach out.'

Mrs Jones nodded, her eyes reflecting both gratitude and understanding. She leaned in closer, 'I will,' she replied. A warm smile graced her lips as she continued, 'And thank you, Officer. I know I can be a bit of a waffler, and even my own family seldom gives me the attention you have today. You're a genuinely nice person. I just hope you can find out what happened to Lizzie.'

As Mrs Jones left the station, Keeley knew exactly who had visited Lizzie on the night she died. She pushed her unfinished sandwich aside and gathered her things. She dialled a number on her phone. When the call was answered, she said, 'Hello, it's PC Cooper. We need to talk.'

51

'Hello, PC Cooper. What can I do for you?'

'Oh, it's you, Mrs Bardwell. Hello. Could I have a word with your husband, please?'

'Could you tell me what this is concerning, officer?'

'I think it would be best if I speak to him directly concerning this matter.'

'If it's regarding my sister, I would appreciate knowing. Is it somehow linked to Lizzie?'

'I think it's best I have this conversation with your husband, it might be nothing.'

'Please tell me. I know it is! He's been acting strangely ever since that night she died —working late, keeping secrets. Call it a wife's intuition, but something has happened.'

Keeley hesitated.

'Alright. As I mentioned, this could be insignificant, but I need to investigate. It concerns Lizzie's neighbour who has now come forward, indicating that she witnessed your husband outside Lizzie's residence on the night of her death, apparently he was shouting and banging on the door.'

'Hold on, that doesn't sound right. I remember he was at work that night,' she countered. 'I called him several times when I found out about Lizzie. I wouldn't take her neighbour's words too seriously, Officer,' Lisa remarked dismissively. 'She tends to be rather erratic and unreliable.'

'Alright, I'll confirm this information. Is your husband around, Mrs Bardwell? I'd appreciate speaking with him about this.'

'He's not at home at the moment.'

Keeley's brow furrowed slightly. 'Is he expected back soon?'

'I have no idea. He's currently in surgery. There's an emergency procedure that he couldn't delay.'

'I'm sorry to hear that, is he okay?' Keeley replied, slightly taken aback by the information.

Lisa paused and then said, 'He's a doctor, didn't you know that?'

'No, I didn't know that. In that case, could you please pass on the message that I called? I'd appreciate talking to him whenever he's free. Thanks a lot.'

Keeley's heart raced as she ended the call. She had a feeling that there was more to this.

She began researching James Bardwell. She scanned the profiles until her eyes landed on one: "Anaesthetist, Lead Consultant, Dr James Bardwell."

James Bardwell's connection to Lizzie and his employment at the same hospital as Sierra seemed too coincidental. Why had James Bardwell been banging on his sister-in-law's door on the night of her demise?

With her decision made, she stepped into Sergeant Parker's office and saw him slouched at his desk, surrounded by reports. He looked up as she entered.

'Sir, I've made a breakthrough,' she declared. 'I suspect a potential link between Mr Bardwell and Lizzie's demise. We need to bring in Mr Bardell for questioning.'

'The brother-in-law? I think it's a strong no. We cannot do that. He was the one who made the complaint about you to the coroner.'

Keeley's shock was evident on her face, 'But, Sir. I'm onto something here—'

'I have already instructed you to let go of this case, Keeley. It has been closed as a suicide. No more questions. Drop it,' he commanded firmly.

Sergeant Parker looked at Keeley with a stern expression.

'Respectfully, sir, I can't merely abandon this. There are too many unanswered questions, and I believe there is more to this case than meets the eye. I owe it to the two victims and their families to uncover the truth.'

Sergeant Parker's face hardened, his patience

wearing thin. 'You are crossing a line, PC Cooper. I won't tolerate insubordination. Consider this your final warning. Any more and you will be suspended!'

Keeley's shoulders slumped as she listened to Sergeant Parker. 'Understood, sir,' she responded before exiting his office.

'Is everything okay, mate?' Sergeant Morgan called out to her.

Keeley sighed. 'No. He's a stubborn old man who spends his day behind a desk. I'm so close to this, I cannot give up now. I know what I've got to do.'

Sergeant Morgan nodded. 'You're a determined person, Keeley. Be careful.'

With a brief but reassuring smile, Keeley nodded.

Keeley's phone buzzed in her pocket, interrupting her thoughts. She frowned and ignored it. She had a case to solve.

52

Cecil parked his car down the street from Tulips. He scanned the surroundings, his mind racing with thoughts of Kay's safety.

The previous day's events weighed heavily on his mind. He hoped his actions had dissuaded Frank, but he couldn't afford complacency. Kay had become essential to his life, filling a void he had felt for years.

As Cecil sat in his car, his mind wandered back to his mid-20s, a time when he was engaged to a woman named Marie. Marie struggled with Cecil's long absences while he was serving in the Navy. Loneliness led her into an affair, which shattered their relationship. Cecil ended their engagement, disillusioned with love. Since then, he has chosen a life of solitude.

Before his watch began, he visited Thomas and gave him the recording of Frank's confession from the previous night. He instructed Thomas to take the recording and the CCTV footage to PC Cooper at the Lowestoft Police Station if anything happened to him or Kay in retaliation.

As he sat in his car, watching the day unfold uneventfully, he let out a yawn and rubbed his eyes, squinting as the sun began to set. Cecil wiggled in his seat and rubbed his lower back.

Kay stepped out of the shop's front door, her red curls blowing in the breeze. He leaned forward in his chair and squinted. She darted her eyes around nervously before getting into her car and driving away. Cecil checked his pocket watch and waited a few minutes before leaving himself.

Upon returning home, he walked through the door to hear the ringing of his landline in the kitchen.

He hastened to answer it, anticipating a concerned family member.

'Hello, Whitford & Sons Ltd,' Cecil answered in his usual professional manner.

'Mr Whitford, it's Dr Pilkington. I've been trying to reach PC Cooper. There's something important to discuss. I believe I'm the one that has stumbled upon a murder this time.' Dr Pilkington's voice carried an undertone of urgency and concern.

'Go ahead, Dr Pilkington. I'm all ears.'

'Well... I received a male body today. Nothing seemed out of the ordinary initially, but during the examination, I noticed a peculiar skin puncture between his hallux and phalange—

indicative of an injection. He flatlined due to the accident, but the presence of the puncture raises questions. Don't you think?'

'Was he a diabetic?' Cecil enquired.

'Let me see. No, he's not diabetic, according to his records. Mr Robert Hoskins died of cardiac arrest. But it's strange how a stable patient would tank so suddenly when you read the patient's chart.'

'Wait... What did you just say?' Cecil interrupted.

'Died of cardiac arrest.'

'No! Not that, his name. You said it was Robert Hoskins, right?'

'Yes, Robert Hoskins, aged 37, died of cardiac arrest at Ipswich Hospital.'

Cecil's mind raced as he realised the implications. 'Dammit!

'What are you rambling on about, Mr Whitford?'

'I was there when he died. He dated Lizzie Hargrave and was connected to the young nurse's suicide. This is bad. I need to tell PC Cooper.'

'Oh no, that can't be a coincidence. I'll make sure to keep you updated if I find anything else, Mr Whitford.'

Dr Pilkington's concern echoed through the phone as Cecil hung up. Dread set in, and the town's mounting deaths were unsettling. Lost in thought, he noticed a voicemail—a call missed while talking to Dr Pilkington. He played the message.

53

He observed the patient on the bed with a detached look, his expression void of emotion. It would be just another routine task, numbing the young man's pain with a local anaesthetic. The broken leg and mangled hand were a puzzle, he wondered what kind of troublemaker had orchestrated this mess.

As the anaesthetic took effect, he discarded his gloves and stepped out of the room. After a moment, he stood in the corridor, observing the patient board. The sight of a certain name triggered flashbacks of a recent event, and a wry smile appeared on his face.

A threatening message to expose his secrets had launched the sinister plot.

Scanning the board for his next patient, he froze, his eyes locked on another name, a patient in the Trauma and Orthopaedics ward.

Curious, he made his way up the stairs to the

ward.

Upon entering the ward, his eyes darted around the room, scanning each bed. He approached the last bed, but a lone police officer obstructed his view. He moved to the neighbouring bed, scanning their monitor, while sneaking a glance at the other bed. It was the very individual who had been blackmailing him.

He hesitated, his heart pounding. He wiped away the sweat that had formed on his forehead with his lab coat sleeve. Then, he made his way to the storage cupboard. Inside, he unlocked the medical supply cabinet and removed a small, clear glass bottle with a rubber stopper.

'Nurse. Could you assist me with the patient over there? I need you to change his catheter.'

'Sure, I can help you with that.'

He watched as the nurse made her way to the bed, momentarily speaking with the police officer who left. The nurse deftly drew the curtain. She exited the area moments later and made her way to another bed.

He smoothly swept aside the curtain. He withdrew the insulin and a syringe from his pocket, trembling as he removed the cap and held it up to the light. Tiny bubbles floated in the clear liquid. He took a deep breath and depressed the plunger, forcing out the air.

Turning to the unconscious patient, he inserted the needle into their vein, slowly pushing the insulin into the man's body.

'Dr Bardwell? Hello, are you there? Is my patient prepared for surgery?'

'What? Oh, yes! They're prepared, Dr Patel.'

'Good, it's about time,' Dr Patel remarked with a hint of impatience. 'The real doctors can get to work now.' He shot a condescending glance at Dr Bardwell. 'While you just stand around looking gormless.'

He just smiled back at Dr Patel, his expression inscrutable and his thoughts hidden behind the façade of professionalism. An unsettling thought flitted through his mind—imagining what he'd like to do to Dr Patel he headed back to his office.

As he entered his office and turned on the light, he froze. His eyes widened slightly, 'Can I help you?' he asked.

'Yes, Mr Bardwell, we need to talk about a few things. I have some more questions to ask about Lizzie.'

54

'Mr Whitford...I apologise for calling so late, but I don't know what to do. My boss won't listen. It's about Lizzie and Sierra's deaths. The situation has become a nightmare. I thought we had solved it, with Rob Hoskins behind it all, but new evidence has come to light that suggests otherwise. Lisa's husband, Dr. Bardwell, is a doctor at Ipswich Hospital. Hear me out—on the night of Lizzie's death, a neighbour witnessed him pounding on her door, shouting aggressively. I need to talk to him, just in case. I know this sounds crazy, I mean he can't have murdered his sister-in-law. Could he? Don't worry about it. I am sure I am not in any danger, I don't know why I'm telling you this. Just ignore what I am saying. Have a good evening.'

PC Cooper's message reminded him of one of his fellow Navy comrades who had taken his own life one night. The man had been going through a rough time; his wife had filed for divorce, and he was struggling with the idea of losing his family.

They had been friends for several years, having trained together and gone on several deployments. He had always been a cheerful and outgoing person, but something had changed in him. One night, his friend confided in him. Cecil had ignored his cry for help and told him things would work out. One day, he received a call from the base chaplain, asking him to come to the barracks. When he arrived, he found Nigel's body hanging from a noose in his room.

It was a devastating sight, and he felt a wave of emotions. He couldn't believe that his friend had taken his own life, and he felt guilty that he had not noticed the signs of his distress—the warning signs were there, but he never acted on them.

Since that moment, he has vowed to trust his instincts and will do everything in his power to help others through their troubles. He knew that he couldn't save everyone, but he would do everything in his power to try.

Standing in the kitchen, clutching Nigel's pocket watch, Cecil replayed PC Cooper's message in his mind. The truth was finally coming to light. Dr Bardwell's connection to Lizzie and the hospital where Sierra had been treated, coupled with the marks on their bodies and the insulin found in Rob's system, solidified Cecil's theory. It all pointed to Dr Bardwell.

Cecil dialled PC Cooper's number and the dial tone rang in his ear. The first ring, the second ring, the third ring. He pressed the voicemail button and left a hurried voicemail, his voice laced with concern. Frustration washed over him as he slammed the phone back into its holder.

Cecil rushed to his car, keys in hand. His thoughts were focused on one thing: finding PC Cooper and uncovering the truth.

55

'I don't understand why you're still looking into this.'

'I understand that you're frustrated, but I need to ask you a few more questions. Were you at Lizzie's house on the night of her death?'

James's heart pounded in his chest as he wondered how Keeley knew about his visit to Lizzie's house. Did Rob inform the police?

'Maybe I did visit her that night. I don't remember much,' James responded.

Undeterred, Keeley leaned forward, her voice steady. 'There's a witness,' she said calmly, 'who recounted seeing you, your voice raised, your demeanour intense. You were locked in an argument with Lizzie.'

James's voice wavered slightly, his fingers tapping a restless rhythm on the table. He met Keeley's stare, his eyes narrowing and his jaw clenching.

'That does sound familiar. I think we had a disagreement, now that I recall. It was about money. She owed us thousands. Lisa was constantly giving her money. So I went there to talk to her about it. Yes, it's all coming back to me now.'

Taking a deep breath, Keeley asked the next question, her voice steady. 'Tell me about your relationship with Lizzie. Were you two romantically involved?'

James closed his eyes and drew a long breath. His hands clenched into fists. 'Absolutely not,' he replied. 'It was civil. We didn't interact much, but we didn't have any problems either. I already told you that I went to her house that night to discuss money. There was nothing romantic between us.'

Keeley persisted, a knowing glint in her eyes as she pressed further. 'I have to ask, have you ever been unfaithful to your wife?'

His lips tightened into a thin line, his retort dripping with defensiveness. 'You have some nerve accusing me of that.'

'Do you deny acting unfaithful? In fact, I myself saw you at the Paradise Escape Lounge intimately with someone recently,' Keeley countered, maintaining eye contact.

James responded with a dismissive shrug. 'So what? That doesn't mean anything.'

Undeterred, Keeley continued her questioning, bringing up Sierra Watson, a nurse who worked at the hospital. James visibly tensed, his expression turning cold. 'I don't know what you're talking about.'

'I just need to know the truth,' Keeley said.

'I've given you my answer. I had nothing to do with Lizzie's death. If that's all, I've got tasks to do. As for your investigation, officer, it seems like a futile pursuit.'

'Thank you for your time, Mr Bardwell. I plan to speak to your wife further and your colleagues. Just to check the facts of this discussion.'

'Fine, I have nothing to hide. On your way, officer.'

As Keeley walked away, James turned his attention back to the computer screen. With an audible burst of rage, he slammed his fist into the keyboard, scattering the plastic keys.

<u>56</u>

Keeley walked back to her car, thinking about Mr Bardwell. She knew he was hiding something, his manner was far too defensive. She decided to speak to the witness again, hoping to learn more about what they had seen that night.

On her way to her car, Keeley passed a group of teenagers gathered by a nearby bench, laughing and joking around. A woman who was struggling to wrangle her toddler into a car seat. An elderly couple slowly walked hand-in-hand towards the hospital. Keeley wondered about their lives.

Her phone beeped, startling her. Opening the message, she saw that her parking time was almost up. She quickened her pace.

Keeley squinted in the poorly lit car park, searching for her white Fiat 500. She walked up and down the rows, her eyes scanning the licence plates. After a few moments, she spotted her car and hurried towards it.

She slid into the driver's seat and closed the door. Her phone continued to beep. She glanced at the display and saw that she had missed calls from an unfamiliar number. She frowned and checked her voicemail.

'First new message'

'Good evening, PC Cooper. Mr Whitford here. Nothing too pressing, but I'd appreciate it if you could give me a call when you have a moment. It might be nothing. Thanks.'

Keeley pressed the other voicemail icon for the other message.

'Second new message received today...'

'Mr Whitford called again. When you get a minute, can you call me back? It's quite urgent. It's about Rob Hoskins. I believe he was murdered. I think... I think you might be in real trouble. Please, hurry—'

She quickly dialled the caller back, her fingers trembling so badly that she dropped the phone at her feet. Bending in her chair, she grabbed it and held it to her ear, waiting for the call to connect. Out of the corner of her eye, she saw a dark figure moving towards her car. She strained her eyes to make out their features.

Nearing closer, their footsteps tapped the concrete and then came to a stop. She reached for the car lock, but before she could turn it, the door was yanked open abruptly.

A strong hand grabbed her around the throat,

she kicked and punched wildly but her seatbelt restrained her. She tried to scream but a handkerchief covered her nose and mouth. The pungent scent of ether-like chemicals filled her nostrils, its sweet taste causing her to gag. She tried again to undo her seatbelt, but her fingers were fumbling and weak.

Keeley's vision blurred and her eyelids drooped. Her last conscious sight was James Bardwell's face, his eyes burning with hatred.

57

Cecil's grip tightened on the wheel as he sped down the A12 road. He couldn't stop thinking about PC Cooper's cryptic voicemail. What had she meant by 'danger'? Was she in trouble? As he approached the hospital, he felt uneasy.

He pulled into Car Park F. The lights were dim, and the only sound was the wind rustling through the trees as he exited his vehicle. As he walked to the parking metre, he spotted Keeley's white Fiat 500 pass him.

Cecil peered into the car. PC Cooper slumped in the passenger seat, her head resting against the window. The driver sat stiffly, their face expressionless, their eyes locked straight ahead.

Cecil frowned as he watched the car speed away, he didn't recognise the driver. PC Cooper's voicemail echoed in his mind. Something was very wrong. He had to do something, but what?

Cecil's heart pounded in his chest as he made

his way back to his hearse. Without hesitation, he fired up the engine and pulled out of the car park. He followed the Fiat 500 on the A12 road, maintaining a distance but ensuring he didn't lose sight of it.

Why was Keeley in that car with that man? Was she in danger? Was that James Bardwell driving? These thoughts worried him, but he pushed them away and followed them for an hour until they arrived in Lowestoft, crossing over the retractable footbridge on the A12.

Cecil maintained a discreet distance as the Fiat 500 slowed and turned onto Tonning Street. Suddenly a car began pulling off his drive, blocking the road ahead.

'What's the matter with people? Don't they know how to drive?' Cecil said.

Eventually, he set off again, turning down the same street he had seen PC Cooper's car head down.

Cecil slammed on the brakes, his tyres screeching on the pavement. He had lost sight of the white Fiat. He craned his neck out the window, scanning the street in all directions, but the car was nowhere to be seen.

He put the car in reverse and backed up to the previous junction. He stopped the car and looked around again. The Fiat was gone.

He clenched his fists in frustration. 'Damn it, where have you gone!' he muttered under his breath.

58

Closing the front door behind him, James entered the narrow hallway. He briefly looked down at the police officer lying on the floor before stepping over her.

James's gloved hands moved quickly and efficiently as he searched through the kitchen drawers, until his fingers closed around the handle of a small kitchen knife and he pulled it out, studying the polished blade with satisfaction, he left it on the kitchen top.

After climbing the stairs, James scoured the upstairs rooms. The house comprised two bedrooms - a sparsely furnished guest room and another brimming with furniture. At the end of the hallway, he reached the last door. It creaked as he opened it, revealing a tired-looking bathroom. James turned the tap, old pipes clattering as water slowly filled the bath.

As he headed back, he was startled by a low

groan coming from downstairs.

James froze in the middle of the stairs, his heart pounding in his chest. He held his breath and listened intently, but there was nothing else. He slowly started to move again, his footsteps tentative. Then he heard another sudden groan.

He rushed downstairs and saw Keeley sitting upright on the floor, her head hanging low and her eyes unfocused. She tried to stand, but her legs wobbled and she fell to her hands and knees. She began to crawl towards the front door, her movements slow and laboured.

James's feet pounded on the hardwood floor as he dashed into the kitchen. He snatched the knife from the counter, his fingers closing around the handle with a fierce grip. He spun around and raced back into the hallway.

'Take another step, and you'll regret it,' James commanded.

Keeley looked at him, panic on her face. She tried to climb to her feet and held onto the wall, working to steady herself.

'You think you c-can...j-just g-get...away with th-th-th-this?' Keeley blinked her eyes rapidly, clutching her head with her hand. 'I know who you are now, and...and others will too. I won't be some helpless...victim,' she stuttered.

James's grip on the knife tightened. 'It's just you and me,' James said with a smirk, his 'No one's coming to save you. Now, get upstairs!'

As she walked towards the stairs, she glanced

back at James.

'Let's go!' He emphasised his words with a firm shove, guiding her towards the staircase.

Walking towards the stairs, Keeley snatched up the table lamp and hurled it at James. He instinctively raised his arms to protect himself, but the lamp collided with his forearms with a sickening thud.

Keeley's shoulders squared and her chin lifted as she landed a powerful kick to his knee, sending him sprawling to the floor. The knife spun out of his hand across the floor.

Seeing her chance, Keeley sprinted towards the front door, her heart pounding in her chest.

But James, driven by a mix of desperation and fury, was swift to respond. He retrieved the knife and lunged forward, his fingers closing around her arm in a vice-like grip, yanking her back with force. He waved the knife towards her.

'You stupid bitch! Big mistake,' he hissed. His eyes were wide and his nostrils flaring. 'You really think you can escape me? You'll pay dearly for this. Try anything else, and I'll finish you right now.'

With a reluctant nod, she uttered, 'Fine. I understand.'

'Now, let's try this again. Head upstairs!'

Keeley reluctantly climbed the stairs with James close on her heels, the blade poised for action. With a nod, he indicated the bathroom at the far end of the landing, with the sound of running water echoing.

She hesitated at the entrance, her body trembling with a mix of fear and uncertainty. She took a cautious glance over her shoulder, attempting to gauge the situation.

Suddenly she was brutally shoved from behind, sending her crashing down onto the cold tile floor.

'Get up!' James commanded, grabbing hold of her hair.

Keeley's voice quivered slightly. 'Why did you kill Lizzie and Sierra?'

Annoyance flickered across James's face, a sinister smile fading as his eyes flashed with aggression. 'I've no time for your questions,' he retorted.

'If you're going to kill me, you can at least tell me that!'

They locked eyes.

'Why did you kill them, James?' she insisted, her eyes unwavering.

He sighed heavily, 'Fine!' he snapped, his eyes rolling back in his head. 'Because things were getting complicated. Lizzie found out about my affair with Sierra. It was endangering my marriage and therefore, my wealth. If I got divorced, I would be left with nothing! I couldn't risk that. I had to get rid of them both to safeguard everything I've built. That conniving, money-grabbing bitch Lizzie even tried to blackmail me.'

'What happens next, then?'

James leaned over her, 'Your fate? You're going to commit suicide.'

Her jaw dropped and her eyes widened in fear as she clutched her arms around her body.

He smiled cruelly. 'Picture it—you're going to stage your own suicide as a young police officer who was overcome by the trauma of her job and took her own life. Isn't it poetic?'

<u>59</u>

Keeley's heart pounded in her chest as she scanned the room, her eyes darting back and forth. She knew she needed to find a way out, but all she saw were solid walls and the closed door. Her skin felt clammy and her palms were sweaty.

She turned to face James, her eyes meeting his. Slowly, she nodded.

'Good. Let's proceed,' James said. His cold blue eyes locked onto hers with an unsettling intensity. 'Now, undress and get in!'

She crossed her arms tightly over her chest, creating a protective barrier, shielding herself from the distasteful proposition.

'No. You can't force me,' she said, lifting her chin resolutely.

James' face twisted in anger, his grip tightening around the knife. He moved closer, 'You don't have a choice,' he hissed. 'Defy me, and you'll regret it.' He swung the knife dangerously close to her neck, leaving no room for disobedience. 'Now do as I say!'

Keeley stared at him, then reluctantly began to undress. As she removed her top first, her eyes never left him.

While keeping his eyes on her, he switched the knife to his other hand, withdrew the remaining Propofol bottle, placed it on the floor, and with his free hand, retrieved a syringe. The clear liquid filled the syringe.

Keeley's gaze laser-focused on James, her muscles tensing as she propelled herself at him. Fear and willpower coursed through her, lending an almost superhuman speed to her movements as they collided with a thud, bodies crashing to the ground in a whirlwind of motion.

The knife slipped from James's grasp, clattering across the floor in the dim light of the room.

Keeley's fists moved like lightning, fuelled by a fierce resolve to survive. 'Take that, you bastard!' Keeley yelled angrily. Each punch was a raw expression of her grit, the impact of her knuckles against James's form punctuating the air.

'Get off me, you bitch!' James spat out, his voice a mix of anger and desperation as he struggled beneath her. Desperately raising his arms to try and shield most of Keeley's strikes, he eventually wrestled her off of him.

In the chaotic struggle, Keeley noticed a glint come into view—a syringe.

James's hand darted and the needle found its mark in her thigh. The cool touch of metal met her skin, sending an immediate chill through her veins as the drug took hold.

Her limbs began to feel heavy, as if gravity itself had increased its pull. The edges of her vision blurred and the room seemed to tilt and waver in a surreal distortion. The battle cries that had filled the air turned into muted gasps, her fight against the drug's effects becoming an uphill struggle. Despite the drug's numbing effects, she fought to continue her flurry of punches, but her fists felt like lead, each strike slower and weaker than the last. As her surroundings grew dim and her body rebelled, Keeley collapsed onto the cold tiled floor.

As Keeley's consciousness wavered and dimmed, James's voice cut through the haze with a chilling finality. 'You should have listened. Good riddance, PC Cooper.'

James forcibly tore away the remainder of her clothing, disregarding any sense of dignity or respect. He lifted her limp form and callously deposited it into the cold, unforgiving embrace of the bathtub.

With her unconscious body now entirely at his mercy, he reached into the bathwater and grabbed her wrist with an unyielding grip. The knife gleamed ominously in his other hand, its blade poised over her wrist, ready to strike.

Seizing the opportune moment, he executed

his plan. With one swift stroke, the knife sliced into her flesh, releasing a torrent of crimson. The blood spilled out, mingling with the water in a macabre display.

He watched with a twisted sense of satisfaction, as if orchestrating a morbid spectacle.

Carefully, he switched the knife to her other hand and closed her fingers around it.

He stepped back, surveying his work with a twisted satisfaction. 'There,' he muttered to himself, 'Nice work, PC Cooper.'

Glancing at his watch, he began racing around the house, scrubbing down every surface and object he had touched since entering. Returning to the bathroom, he took one final glance before going downstairs and exiting the house.

He emerged onto the street, clutching his chest and letting out rapid breaths, he glanced back at the house. Would this mislead the authorities long enough? he thought to himself.

Confident his latest ruse would buy him time to escape, he knew there was no return. The hospital parking lot's surveillance cameras likely captured the evening's events, so he had no choice but to vanish.

<u>60</u>

Cecil weaved his way through parked cars and down each street, his eyes darting back and forth, searching for the Fiat 500.

The tyres squealed as Cecil slammed on the brakes, coming to a jarring halt in front of the Fiat 500. He had found it.

He manoeuvred into a narrow space nearby and leapt out. His eyes darted from house to house. He was sure that they had gone into one of them, but he didn't know which one.

Cecil froze, his heart pounding in his chest. The sound of a door opening had startled him. He ducked behind a bush, holding his breath. He peered through the leaves, watching as a tall, broad-shouldered man stepped out of the house. Cecil squinted, trying to make out the man's features in the dim light. Was it James Bardwell?

The man shifted from foot to foot, glancing over his shoulder nervously. He checked his watch, then turned and walked away, his long strides carrying him down the street in the opposite direction.

Cecil rose from cover and pressed his back against the wall. He slinked through the shadows, his eyes fixed on the unknown man. His muscles tensed as he fought the urge to chase after him. He froze; the man was moving away, getting farther and farther. He turned to follow him, but stopped. He looked back at the house he had left, a pang of guilt in his chest.

He crept up to the front door, listening for any signs of activity. Silence. He crouched down, he squinted through the letterbox into the gloom, his eyes straining to pick out any movement. The only sound coming from the house was the ticking of a clock in the hallway.

He reached out and gently tried the doorknob. It was locked. Cecil frowned. He had been expecting this, but it was still disappointing. He studied the door for a moment, taking in the details. It was a solid oak door, with a brass push-down doorknob.

Cecil reached into his wallet and pulled out a credit card. He inserted the credit card into the gap between the door and the frame and tried to jimmy the lock. But the card was too flimsy and bent in the middle. He cursed under his breath. 'Damn it, automatic deadbolt!'

He knew that it would be difficult to pick an automatic deadbolt lock with a credit card. He would need a special tool for that. There were also no accessible ground-level windows. He sighed and put the credit card back in his wallet.

He needed to find another way to get inside. He stepped back and scanned the front of the house but found no other entry points. He glanced at the alleyway to the side of the house. He wondered if the houses on this block had back gardens. Sneaking in through there might work. He raced down the narrow alleyway, counting the houses he passed until he reached the right one.

Swiftly retracing his path where he had parked, he opened the boot and delved into a compact red toolbox. After some searching, he produced an orange flathead screwdriver and returned to the garden gate. A quick assessment of the garden gate revealed it lacked a high-security lock.

He wedged the screwdriver between the knuckle and pin, and began tapping the handle downward with his other hand. The pin became loose. He repeated the process with the bottom hinge until the gate was free. He lifted it off its hinges with care, making as little noise as possible, and rested it against the wall.

Entering the rear garden, he quickly scanned the area. It was mainly a neglected lawn with red-brick flower beds. He approached the rear door and tried the handle. Locked, dammit! He spotted the key on the other side.

He grabbed one of the red bricks from a pile nearby, likely left over from building the flower beds. He wrapped his suit jacket around it, then slammed it into the window. The glass shattered. He held his breath, listening intently for any signs of neighbours being alerted. All he could hear was the wind whistling through the trees and the distant barking of a dog. No lights came on in the neighbouring houses.

Satisfied, he reached in to turn the key to unlock the door. The kitchen he entered was pristine and a faint scent of citrus lingered in the air. He followed the soft glow of light into the hallway.

Quietly, he began ascending the stairs, but each step caused the floorboards to creak, making it difficult to be truly stealthy. Unsure if the man he had seen earlier might have returned or had an accomplice, he didn't want to alert anyone else who might be in the house. Reaching the landing, his attention was drawn to the bathroom, where he could see a hand loosely hanging over the side of the bathtub.

61

As he burst into the bathroom, the scene that greeted him was beyond belief.

PC Cooper lay motionless in the bath, her blood staining the water. A deep gash marred her wrist, and blood slowly oozed along the tub's edge.

Urgency surged within him; he knelt beside her and pressed his index and middle fingers against the side of her neck. Simultaneously, he fumbled for his pocket watch, measuring the seconds as he realised her pulse was weak.

Without a moment's hesitation, Cecil sprang into action. He squatted down beside the bathtub and placed his arms under Keeley's armpits. He tried to lift her, but her weight was too much for him. He gritted his teeth and tried again, this time heaving with all his might.

Finally, he was able to lift Keeley out of the bath. His suit jacket was soaked in the crimson-tinted water as he hoisted her above the tub's edge and onto the floor mat. The effort etched lines of strain on his face and his cheeks flushed with the exertion.

Quickly assessing the situation, he wrapped her in a large towel to keep her warm and, to prevent further blood loss, he pressed a small towel against her bleeding wrist, his fingers slick with her blood. Holding her arm up above her head, as he had been trained to do, he ensured blood flow would slow. Her body twitched, and she groaned, but he could tell she was unconscious, likely due to the drugs that must have been administered.

A deep sense of urgency gripped him. He knew he needed to get her to safety as soon as possible. He briefly considered calling an ambulance but doubted it would be the best course of action given they would not reach her in time.

Gripping her under the arms, he lifted her from the floor, his muscles straining. He navigated the hallway slowly, his lower back aching. The old wooden stairs groaned beneath their weight. When he reached the living room, he gently lowered her to the sofa.

He fumbled with the key, his fingers clumsy and numb from the cold water. The key didn't turn, so he tried again, harder this time. His muscles tensed with effort, but the key wouldn't budge. He let out a heavy sigh. He turned the key with all his might, his jaw clenched in determination. The lock finally clicked open, and he breathed a sigh of relief. He flung open the door.

Returning to the lounge, he reassessed her pulse. Though faint, it was still there. She was tougher than she looked, he thought, a glimmer of hope amidst the chaos. He had to carry her outside and struggled through the doorway.

He unlocked the hearse whilst trying to maintain his balance. He swung open the rear door, and she began to groan.

'You won't... g-get... away with this, James!' Keeley murmured groggily.

'PC Cooper, it's me! Mr Whitford! I'm going to get you to the hospital,' he said, as he lifted her up.

She drifted in and out of consciousness, her voice barely audible.

Carefully settling her on the back seat, he fastened the seatbelt securely around her waist.

Hurrying to the driver's side, he climbed in and started the engine. Urgency propelled him forward as he pressed down on the accelerator, determined to reach their destination in time.

Mr Whitford's grip on the steering wheel was firm, his foot pressing down on the accelerator as he weaved through traffic. He was acutely aware of the speedometer creeping past the limit, but the urgency of the situation eclipsed any concern for traffic laws. Thankfully the roads were relatively clear this time of time, but he was met with the occasional blaring of car horn as he weaved in and out of traffic.

'Urgh... What? Where... am I?' Keeley's voice quivered from the back seat.

Cecil half-turned his head, his attention briefly shifting from the road to PC Cooper. 'PC Cooper. It's me, Mr Whitford. I'm going to get you to the hospital. You've lost a lot of blood. Listen to me, you need to focus on staying awake,' he urged gently.

'Mr Whitford... Oh god, he... he tried to kill me!' Keeley's voice quivered.

'You're safe now, I got to you just in time.' He maintained his focus on the road.

'It was James Bardwell! He's a doctor at the hospital. He's... married to Lizzie's sister, Lisa. He's the one who... who killed them...' Her voice faded as she spoke, slipping back into unconsciousness.

'You have to stay with me!' he implored, his urgency evident. 'Why did he do it? Why did he kill them?'

As silence hung for a moment, he half-turned towards her, his concern etched on his face.

'PC Cooper, listen carefully. I need to know your blood type. It's crucial that I know before we get to the hospital.'

Still no response.

'PC Cooper... PC Cooper... wake up! This is important. What is your blood type?'

'Mmm... what? Mmm... it's A,' came a faint,

meek voice from the back of the car.

'Thank you. How are you doing back there?'

He noticed her complexion growing paler by the second in the rearview mirror.

Glancing at the picture of him and Nigel on the dashboard, he gripped the steering wheel tightly, the engine growling as Cecil pressed the accelerator to the floor. The tyres screeched as he took turns too sharply.

Keeley groaned and slumped against the door, her eyes closing.

Cecil glanced at her again in the rearview mirror.

'Hang on, PC Cooper!' he shouted. 'We're almost there!'

__62__

Cecil's tyres screeched as he braked hard in the no-parking zone in front of the hospital. He swung open the door and heaved PC Cooper out. He staggered under her weight, but he didn't dare slow down. He hurried towards the hospital entrance, his heart pounding in his chest.

The harsh fluorescent lights of the hospital blinded him as he entered. He paused for a moment, disoriented. He looked down at his blood-stained clothes and the young police officer in his arms. Her face was pale and her eyes were closed. He knew he had to act quickly.

Panicked faces and a few gasps snapped him back to the task at hand.

He hurried towards the reception desk. Before he could make it, a stern-looking nurse marched up to him and said in a firm voice, 'What's going on here?'

'PC Cooper, female. She has a deep cut to

the wrist, resulting in significant blood loss. I've performed basic first aid to stop the bleeding, but she needs an immediate blood transfusion or she won't survive. We're wasting time she doesn't have!'

'Sir, you cannot go any further. I am Nurse Ava, we will get her the care she needs, but you can't come in here demanding this and that.'

'Please, let's not waste time with formalities. I specialise in trauma and know what I'm doing,' Cecil explained urgently, locking eyes with Nurse Ava.

Nurse Ava rolled her eyes and guided him hurriedly towards the treatment area. Cecil followed, carrying PC Cooper.

They quickly prepared a bed for her. Nurse Ava asked for her blood type.

'A. Please hurry!' Cecil replied.

Nurse Ava left momentarily and returned carrying several blood bags containing a bright red liquid. 'I just need to grab another of my colleagues to help, I won't be gone for a moment.'

Cecil snatched them and the cannula out of her hands.

'Sir, you cannot do that. Please give those back!' Nurse Ava exclaimed in annoyance.

'You're taking too long—time she doesn't have,' Cecil replied. With practised ease, he inserted the tube into PC Cooper's vein, initiating the blood transfusion.

'Done,' he said, stepping back to assess his

work. It had been a close call, but he was relieved that PC Cooper had received the much-needed blood just in time. Cecil glanced at PC Cooper in the hospital bed and noticed Nurse Ava's sour expression as she stood with crossed arms, glaring at him.

'Sir, I understand you may know what you're doing, but you cannot just come in here and take over like that,' she scolded.

'I did what was needed to save her life,' Cecil retorted, feeling a tinge of irritation at Nurse Ava's resistance.

'Well, I'm still going to have to ask you to leave the ward!' she said firmly.

Cecil sighed and nodded, acknowledging that he had caused a disturbance.

As he headed back to the lifts, he replayed something PC Cooper said to her 'He is a doctor at Ipswich Hospital'.

He headed to the lifts and descended to the ground floor.

Quickly he took himself into the bathroom and began scrubbing the blood off his hands and face. He buttoned his suit up to hide his blood-soaked white shirt. He didn't look very gentlemanly but at least the receptionist would not call security if they saw him now.

He strolled over to the reception desk, where a tired and bored receptionist was the only one manning the desk at this hour.

'Excuse me, I'm looking for Dr Bardwell'

'Sir, visiting hours are closed, and...'

'Oh, sorry, I didn't make myself clear. He's my son-in-law. My daughter asked me to drop by to pick up his car. He's been complaining that it's been acting up, so I've been asked to take it to the garage for him,' Cecil quickly explained, hoping to avoid any suspicion.

The receptionist appeared slightly apprehensive but wasn't invested enough to question him further. Reluctantly, she provided him with directions to the Anaesthetics department.

'Thank you. Have a nice evening,' Cecil said, attempting to maintain a friendly demeanour.

'I'll try,' the receptionist remarked with a hint of sarcasm.

Cecil's footsteps echoed softly in the empty corridor as he approached the entrance to the Anaesthetics department. Pausing outside the door, he strained his ears for any signs of activity inside. Slowly pushing the door open, he slipped inside and scanned the room for movement. A flickering computer screen caught his attention, drawing him towards the desk. The nurse, engrossed in her work, seemed oblivious to his presence.

'Excuse me, nurse, I was —'

She let out a sharp gasp and her hand flew to her chest. 'You gave me a fright!' she exclaimed. 'I didn't see you there. Can I help you?'

'Sorry to have startled you. I'm looking for Dr

Bardwell,' Cecil said, his voice steady despite his nervousness.

'He's just come back and gone again. If you're quick you might catch him on the way back to the car park. You just missed him,' the nurse replied, barely glancing up from her screen. 'If you're quick, you might catch him.'

He emerged into the car park and scanned the area, his eyes darting around in search of James. There he was, standing next to a black SUV, smoking a cigarette.

Cecil took a deep breath and started walking towards him. He knew he was taking a risk, but he had to find a way to stop James.

James flicked the cigarette butt and climbed into his vehicle, starting the engine.

Cecil sprang into action. He raced back to Angel, the engine roaring to life at his command. He floored the accelerator and sped out of the car park, his headlights cutting through the darkness.

Cecil's eyes locked on the distant red glow of James's car, the only beacon in the night.

63

Cecil hunched over the steering wheel, his eyes glued to the distant tail lights. Shadows danced on the landscape, but he paid them no mind.

Minutes later, he brought his car to a halt, the engine's growl fading into silence.

'Where did you go, you slippery devil?' he said out loud.

Cecil, spotting the distant glow of red tail lights once more, leaned forward in his seat with renewed focus.

A faint smile crossed his face as he saw the tail lights again.

He gripped the steering wheel tightly, ready to continue the pursuit.

Cecil eased the car forward, flicking his headlights off. As he drew closer, he saw the silhouette of a house emerge in the distance. James's car was parked outside. Cecil pulled over to the side of the road, parking in a spot behind a cluster of trees.

Cecil stealthily made his way up the pathway, hugging the sides of the road and blending into the shadows and foliage. From a safe distance, he observed James step out of the car and head inside the house. Though the darkness obscured the man's face, Cecil knew this was the person he had been pursuing all along.

His attention locked onto the front door, Cecil waited until the security light caused an eerie glow, outlining James's figure in the doorway, lugging his possessions to his car.

What was he doing? Is he trying to escape? Cecil contemplated.

Cecil continued to creep up the lane towards the house, the door burst open again, and he recognised Lisa Bardwell as she stormed out. Her shoulders were hunched, her fists clenched reaching James, her hands gesturing wildly as she shouted at him, but Cecil couldn't hear what she was saying.

Suddenly, James let out a roar and lunged at Lisa, grabbing her by the throat. Lisa's eyes widened in fear as she tried to fight him off. James shoved her away, sending her sprawling to the ground. She lay there gasping for air, her face pale with shock.

Cecil took a deep breath and closed his eyes. He reminded himself of why he was here: to bring James to justice. 'I can do this,' Cecil whispered to himself. Cecil opened his eyes and locked onto James in the distance, as he made his way up the lane.

64

Before he could reach the driveway, he heard the black SUV engine fire up.

'Oh, for goodness' sake!' Cecil said. He spun around and ran back to Angel, his breath coming in short gasps. As he ran, he heard the sound of tyres screeching and the roar of the SUV engine getting louder. He glanced over his shoulder and saw the headlights of the SUV approaching, momentarily blinding him. Cecil ducked into the bushes. He held his breath and waited.

A few seconds later, the SUV sped away. Cecil waited before emerging. He sprinted to his car, jumped in, and fired up the engine. He didn't know where James was going, but he knew he had to stay close.

Cecil pursued James down the winding road. Even with his headlights on, it was difficult to see. James's rear lights were barely visible in the distance. Cecil had to stay close.

He gritted his teeth and pressed his foot down on the accelerator. The engine roared and the steering wheel vibrated in his hands.

Just as Cecil thought he had lost James, he saw him around the next bend. He was right on his tail. He could now see James's figure in the driver's seat.

James honked his horn, but this only fueled Cecil's determination. He pressed down on the accelerator, sending his car ramming into the back of James's bumper. Cecil wrestled with the steering wheel as his car nearly spun out of control.

James's car pulled away, creating a car-length distance between them. They approached a sloping hill with a sharp bend sign. Cecil saw James's brake lights ahead as his car began to slow down.

Cecil eased off the accelerator, braking too. But in a split-second decision, he released the brake and veered towards the side of James's car.

The impact was brutal. The two cars collided with such force that Cecil was flung forward, his body crashing into the steering wheel.

Cecil slumped in his seat, his head resting against the steering wheel. His breath came in ragged gasps, and his heart pounded in his chest. He could feel a sharp pain in his forehead, and his vision was blurry. He blinked hard and tried to focus.

He looked around at the interior of his car.

The windshield was cracked. The dashboard was smashed, and the steering wheel was bent. Glass and debris littered the floorboards.

Cecil staggered out of Angel, his back throbbing in pain. He bent over, his hands on his knees, and gasped for breath. He slowly straightened up and looked around.

The other car lay on its side on the other side of the road, its headlights on. The front end was crumpled, and the windshield was shattered. Shards of broken glass littered the road, sparkling in the moonlight.

Cecil took a step forward, then another. He gingerly made his way over to the car. He squinted and peered through the cracks in the windshield, trying to see how James was doing. But the damage was too severe. He couldn't see anything.

He stepped back and frowned. He kicked the windscreen with his heel, but it didn't budge. He kicked it again, harder this time. The glass yielded slightly, but it still didn't crack.

Cecil hobbled back to his car, his injured back throbbing with pain. He opened the boot and retrieved his lug wrench. He gripped the wrench tightly in his hand and advanced towards James's car, his face twisted with rage.

Cecil raised the lug wrench above his head and brought it down with all his might, smashing it into the windshield. The glass shattered, creating a large crater. Cecil peered inside, his eyes widening at the sight of James sprawled on the floor.

'Stop! What do you want? Please, just stop!' James shouted, fear evident in his voice.

Ignoring the pleas, Cecil gripped the lug wrench even tighter, his eyes unyielding. With a swift motion, he swung it back and then launched it forward once again. The force of the blow reverberated through the air as it crashed into the windscreen, sending glass shards flying in every direction.

James attempted to shield himself, but the onslaught was inevitable. Cecil wasn't finished yet. He hooked the remaining windscreen with the wrench and pulled with all his strength. For a brief moment, it seemed as though the glass might hold, but eventually, it succumbed to Cecil's efforts, shattering into countless pieces that cascaded down like a deadly hailstorm.

'Well, well, Mr Bardwell. We finally meet,' Cecil said with cold satisfaction.

'Who the hell are you? You're going to regret this, old man!' James retorted, attempting to mask his fear. 'You won't get away with this! Do you even know who I am?'

Cecil stepped closer, his eyes locked onto James. 'I know exactly who you are and what you've done.'

James's eyes widened. His lips trembled as he tried to speak, but no words came out. Cecil took a step forward, and James flinched. 'I don't know what you're talking about,' James stammered. 'I haven't done anything to you!'

'Oh, but you have,' Cecil said. 'I know what you did to those women. And now, it's time for you to pay the price.'

Without hesitation, Cecil stepped forward and delivered a swift, powerful kick to James's face, causing his head to snap back, and he crumpled unconscious to the floor of the car.

'That's for PC Cooper.'

65

The sound of knocking shattered the station's quietness, pulling Sergeant Parker's attention from his thoughts. Frowning, he left his desk and made his way to the reception area. The knocking persisted, growing louder and more insistent, echoing through the hallway. As he reached the door, he saw a figure standing outside, their features obscured by the light streaming in through the windows.

'We're closed. Come back at 9!' he called out, hoping the visitor would take the hint and leave. But the knocking only intensified, causing the door to shudder under the force of the blows. Frustration welled up within him.

'I'm not in the mood for this. Will you bugger off?' he muttered, his hand reaching for the keys. He unlocked the door and swung it open, ready to confront the disturber of his peace.

'Mr Whitford, what in the blazes are you doing

here?'

'Good morning, Sergeant Parker. Is it a bad time?'

Cecil stood outside the police station entrance, resting against the wall, his suit covered in dirt and grime. His brow bled from a deep cut, and his left eye was bruised and swollen.

'Mr Whitford, what's going on? Look at the state of you! Are you okay?'

'I'm fine. I've got something for you,' Cecil replied cryptically.

Sergeant Parker's jaw tightened as he studied Cecil's battered face. His mind raced as he tried to figure out what was going on.

'What do you mean? Explain yourself!' he asked.

Cecil nodded towards the car park. 'Back there,' he said. 'In Angel.'

Sergeant Parker frowned as he studied the hearse parked outside. The sleek black vehicle was now marred by shattered glass and dents.

'What do you mean, Whitford? What's in your car?' he asked.

Sergeant Parker hesitated for a moment, then turned and followed Cecil.

Sergeant Parker's eyes widened in shock and horror as he pointed to the hearse. 'What in the name of God is that?' he asked. 'You've been warned not to do this again.'

Ignoring the warning, Cecil opened the boot of his car, revealing an injured and bound man.

As Whitford dragged him out, James shouted, 'Will you let me go already?'

Sergeant Parker's eyes studied the battered appearance of the man before him. Then turned to Mr Whitford. 'What are you doing, Mr Whitford? Did you kidnap this man?'

'Allow me to explain,' Cecil said.

'You have sixty seconds before I arrest you,' replied Sergeant Parker.

'This is James Bardwell. He murdered Lizzie Hargrave, Sierra Watson and I believe Rob Hoskins. He tried to flee last night, but I caught up with him.'

'What! The suicides?' Sergeant Parker exclaimed. 'My god, Mr Whitford, this is a mess!'

'It's all true, ask him,' Cecil said.

He gestured to James, who was lying on the floor, bound and bleeding, James's eye was swollen shut and his face was covered in scratches.

James looked up at Sergeant Parker, his eyes wide and red. 'He needs help,' he whispered. 'I'm a doctor. You've got to help me!'

Cecil kicked James in the ribs. James cried out in pain and doubled over.

'You think you can manipulate your way out of this?' Cecil snarled.

James winced. 'Okay, okay,' he said. 'I'll admit it. I killed them all. But the policewoman is alive. She's fine!'

'What policewoman?' asked Sergeant Parker,

turning to Cecil. 'What is he talking about, Whitford?'

Cecil took a deep breath, 'He kidnapped PC Cooper last night and tried to murder her.'

'What?!'

'I got there just in time. She's in the hospital now, but she's going to be okay.'

'PC Cooper is in hospital?' He turned his attention to James on the floor, stepping closer and closer, the look of shock on his face, his fists clenched by his sides. 'You're going down for this, Bardwell. You're going to rot in prison for the rest of your life. You'll never see the sunlight again after I'm done with you.' He grabbed James by the collar and lifted him up, ready to punch him in the face.

Cecil intervened, pulling Sergeant Parker back. 'Easy, Sergeant. He's not worth it. Let the law deal with him,' Cecil said calmly.

Sergeant Parker glared at James, then let him go. Letting out a heavy sigh, he turned back to Cecil.

'I was wrong about you, Mr Whitford. I owe you an apology for doubting you. This case is unlike anything I've encountered before,' Sergeant Parker confessed.

'Don't worry about it. You owe PC Cooper a visit and an apology. She played a crucial role in all of this,' Cecil replied.

'Agreed. She's a remarkable officer,' Sergeant Parker acknowledged.

'Anyway, I'd better get some rest, it's been a long night. The dead never rest, Sergeant. I have a busy day ahead of me, but hopefully, I won't be bringing you any more bodies,' Cecil said with a grin.

Sergeant Parker chuckled. 'Please don't.' He watched as Cecil climbed back into his battered vehicle.

'Now Mr Bardwell, let's get you inside.' said Sergeant Parker, yanking James up from the floor, and forcefully leading him into the station.

66

Keeley lay in the hospital bed, her body sore and her head pounding. The events of the last 24 hours still felt like a bad dream, and she couldn't shake off the fear that James Bardwell might be out there, lurking in the shadows.

As she woke up, the bright lights and bustling sounds of the hospital surrounded her. Memories of James standing over her in the bathtub sent shivers down her spine, but the rest was a hazy blur of fear and pain.

Sitting upright, she surveyed her surroundings. The curtain around her bed was drawn closed, enveloping her in a sense of confinement. Glancing down at her wrist, she noticed it was bandaged, evidence of the harm Bardwell had intended. The painkillers dulled the throbbing ache, leaving her feeling detached and lightheaded. This was coupled with whatever he injected into her unconscious body.

How had she ended up here? What had happened to Bardwell? So many questions echoed in her mind.

Keeley thought about her job and how much she had changed since joining the police force. She had been naive and idealistic at first, but she had quickly learned the harsh realities of the job. She had seen things that she wished she could forget. The weight of it all was heavy on her shoulders, and she longed for a break from the darkness that had consumed her.

A nurse burst through the curtains, breaking her train of thought.

'Good, you're awake. I'm Nurse Chilwell. You're at Ipswich Hospital. Let me check your vitals,' the nurse said, assessing Keeley's temperature, pulse, respiratory rate, and blood pressure. 'Are you hungry?'

'Thank you,' Keeley replied, her voice tinged with weariness. 'I'm not really hungry right now, maybe later.'

'I'll be back to check on you later. Do you want me to leave the curtains open?' Nurse Chilwell asked.

'Yes, please. It feels a bit claustrophobic with them closed. Thank you.' Keeley sighed with relief as the nurse pulled back the curtain and disappeared into the bustling ward.

Alone in her hospital bed, Keeley glanced around the room, observing the other patients.

'Dad, Mum, you're here!' she said.

'Oh, Keels, thank goodness you're okay. We were so worried about you!' Her dad exclaimed, rushing to her side.

'Hi, Dad,' Keeley replied, managing a weak smile.

Her mum followed closely, tears welling up in her eyes. 'We're so sorry, sweetie. We should have believed you,' she choked out.

She furrowed her brow in confusion. 'What are you talking about?'

'We talked to Sergeant Parker, and he told us everything. We feel terrible for not believing you about the suicides,' her mum said.

'We're proud of you for being brave enough to uncover the truth,' her dad added, gently patting her arm.

Keeley blinked back tears, feeling both relieved and drained. 'Thank you, that means a lot,' she whispered, her voice trembling.

'We're here for you, Keeley. Whatever you need, we're here,' her mum said, reaching out to squeeze her hand.

Keeley wiped away her tears and took a deep breath. 'Actually, there's something I need. I want to take some time off work and spend some time with you guys. I need to get away from everything for a while,' she confided, her eyes glassy with tears.

'Of course, Keels. We're more than happy to have you home with us,' her dad replied, his face lighting up with a warm smile.

A wave of relief washed over Keeley as she smiled gratefully. 'Thank you both. I don't know what I'd do without you,' she said.

'We'll always be here for you, Keeley,' her mum assured her, pulling her close in a reassuring hug. 'And we're proud of you, you know? You're going to make a great detective one day. I mean, if that's what you want. Whatever you choose to do with your life, you have my support this time.'

'Thanks, I love you,' Keeley whispered, her voice filled with a mix of exhaustion and gratitude.

Overwhelmed with emotions and the weariness induced by the medication, Keeley found herself drifting off to sleep. Her parents quietly excused themselves, leaving her in the care of the hospital staff.

Hours passed, and as the evening wore on, Sergeant Parker strode into the ward. Keeley stirred from her slumber, her eyes meeting his.

'Keeley, it's good to see you. How are you feeling?'

'I'm doing okay, sir, all things considered. Some pain. I mainly just feel exhausted,' she replied.

'I deeply regret not having believed in you. If only I had listened, this whole situation could have been avoided. I'm truly sorry,' Sergeant Parker said, looking down at his hands.

Keeley smiled, her expression a mix of acceptance and lingering resentment. 'It's okay. I understand why you didn't believe me,' she said.

'I'm sorry for what you've been through, Keeley. You'll be pleased to hear we've arrested Mr Bardwell, and he's confessed to the crimes. You can rest easy knowing that he won't be able to harm you or anyone else ever again.'

A sense of relief washed over Keeley as she listened to the news.

'Thank god! How did you manage to apprehend him?'

'You probably won't believe it, but let me tell you what happened,' Sergeant Parker replied, his voice steady as he recounted the remarkable sequence of events that led to Bardwell's capture. As Keeley listened, a sense of awe and gratitude welled within her, realising the bravery and resourcefulness of Mr Whitford. She marvelled at the twist of fate that had brought him into the picture—a guardian angel in her darkest hour.

Shortly after concluding the story, Sergeant Parker bid farewell and left, leaving Keeley to contemplate the events of the past few days.

Accepting Sergeant Parker's apology brought some closure, but Keeley's heart still held a lingering resentment towards the system that had failed her, nearly costing her life and potentially allowing a dangerous man to escape. She drifted off to sleep once again, her mind filled with hopes of finding further answers and closure in the days to come.

67

PC Cooper logged into her computer and opened her inbox. She had spent the last few weeks recovering from her ordeal with James Bardwell. She sighed heavily as she saw the hundreds of unread emails waiting for her. She took a deep breath and started to sort through them, deleting the spam, forwarding the requests, and replying to the updates. She paused when she saw an email from Sergeant Parker with the subject line "Transfer Approved". She clicked on it and read the message.

She was about to reply to Sergeant Parker when a sudden series of loud thuds startled her.

Alarmed, she walked out into the hall, where the knocking became clearer. It sounded like someone was knocking on the front door of the station, but it was too early for visitors.

She walked through the reception area and looked out through the glass at the car park, but she couldn't see anyone. She cautiously unlocked the door and stepped out into the fresh morning sea breeze.

'Hello, is anyone there?'

'Good morning, officer,' a familiar voice said.

Keeley turned around, ' Hello? Who said that? Is someone there?'

'It's me, Mr Whitford. I'm sorry if I startled you.'

Keeley relaxed a bit. 'Mr Whitford! It's so good to see you. Wait! Please tell me you haven't brought another body.'

'No, no, don't worry.' His smile was reassuring. 'No bodies for you today. I'm here to check on you.'

'Phew, that's a relief. I'm doing okay. Thank you again for what you did. You're like my very own guardian angel.' Keeley's face brightened with a smile.

'Don't worry about it. I'm just glad to see you back at work and take comfort in the fact that we uncovered the truth for the victims' families.'

'I've actually got some exciting news I've just found out about. I've just been granted my transfer request to join Essex Police.'

'Congratulations. We'll be sorry to see you go. If you don't mind me asking, why the change?'

'Well, several reasons, I suppose—the past few months in particular! They made me realise that I can make a difference in people's lives. They have also made me realise how much I miss my family.'

'Family matters. Learn from my mistakes, and don't let your purpose in life be your career. No matter how cynical the world may seem, there will always be good people. People like you will make a difference. I wish you all the best.'

'Thank you again for your help. You saved my life, and we stopped an evil person from ruining more lives.'

'Take care of yourself,' Cecil said before walking back to his car.

'Wait! What's next for you, Mr Whitford?'

'It's funny you asked that. Recent events have made me think about life and what I want to make of it. I've led a quiet and solitary life for too long, with little joy. I'm thinking about retiring and going on a long-overdue trip abroad,' Cecil said, smiling.

As Keeley watched Cecil drive away, she felt a deep sense of gratitude and admiration for the old man.

Walking back to her desk, she grinned and fist-pumped in the air. This was the first step towards a new chapter in her life. As she sat down, her thoughts turned to Mr Whitford. She wondered if he would find happiness and peace in his retirement. Maybe one day she will visit him and thank him again for everything he has done for her.

SPREAD THE WORD AND STAY CONNECTED

Thank you for choosing to read my debut novel. If you've enjoyed the story, I'd appreciate it if you could share it with your friends and family. Word of mouth is a wonderful way to help others discover this book.

If you're on social media and would like to stay updated on future projects, you can follow me there as well. Don't forget to leave a review on: Amazon, Goodreads, or Google Books. Your support feedback means a lot, and I'm grateful for your help in spreading the word about my work.

Thank you for being a part of this journey, and I hope the book continues to bring enjoyment to readers everywhere.

Follow me:
Website - www.domayresauthor.com
Facebook - Dom Ayres Author
Instagram - @domayresauthor

Copyright © 2023 Dominic Ayres
All rights reserved

This is a work of fiction. While reference may be made to actual events or existing locations, the names, characters, places, and incidents are either the product of the author's imagination or are used fictitiously. Any resemblance to any actual persons, living or dead, business establishments, events, or locales is entirely coincidental.

No part of this book may be reproduced, or stored in a retrieval system, or transmitted in any form or by any means, electronic, mechanical, photocopying, recording, or otherwise, without express written permission of the publisher.

ISBN: 9798864753002
Imprint: Independently published

Printed in Great Britain
by Amazon